EARL OF KEYWORTH

A Sweet Regency Romance
For the Love of an Earl, Book Three

COLLETTE CAMERON

Blue Rose Romance®

Sweet-to-Spicy Timeless Romance®

Lord Keyworth inhaled a steadying
breath and shook his dark head again.
"Miss Tolman, I give you my word.
I am *not* asking you to become my mistress."
His cheeks were suspiciously rosy.
As if *he* were actually embarrassed.

Other Collette Cameron Books

For the Love of an Earl
Earl of Wainthorpe
Earl of Scarborough
Earl of Keyworth
Earl of Renshaw

Check out Collette's Other Series
Castle Brides
Heart of a Scot
Seductive Scoundrels
The Culpepper Misses
The Honorable Rogues®
Chronicles of the Westbrook Brides
Highland Heather Romancing a Scot
Daughters of Desire (Scandalous Ladies)

Dedication

For every person who has stayed true to
who you are and what you believe in no matter the cost.
I applaud you for your courage, resolve, and integrity.

Prologue

My darling, not a day goes by that I do not wish we were together. I should have defied Keyworth. I should have been brave and strong and escaped when I knew I carried you, my precious love. But Landry needed me. I was so frightened for him… Can you ever forgive me?

~Letter from the Countess of
Keyworth to her daughter, Lenora.
Never sent. Ripped up and burned.

Faringcroft Park—Earl of Keyworth's Country Seat
Lancaster, England
16 February 1810—Late Evening

Sweat beaded his brow as Landry Audsley, Earl of Keyworth, held his dying mother's cold, frail hand. A roaring fire hissed and snapped angrily in the hearth. Regardless, the Countess of Keyworth shivered, her feeble form racked by chills.

The suffocating heat fairly choked Landry, making it impossible to breathe. Or perhaps it was the unshed tears constricting his throat and cramping his ribs that made the simple task of drawing air into his lungs difficult.

He tenderly drew another blanket from the foot of the bed over his mother's emaciated form.

Always slight of build, his once pretty-as-a-pansy mother had wasted away these past months until only a shell of the woman he adored remained. She was only two-and-forty—much, *much* too young to die.

"I love you, Landry," she said, reaching out to graze his cheek.

A sob caught in Landry's throat and, with grim resolve, he quashed the evidence of his heartbreak.

"I love you too, Mama."

He nearly strangled on the five short words. There was so much more he yearned to say.

His mother was all that was gentle and sweet, compassionate and kind. The opposite of the coldhearted, mercenary blighter she had entered into an arranged marriage with. The previous earl had preceded her in death only last year, and within months she had also fallen ill.

So bloody, bloody unfair.

Providence. Destiny. Fate. Whatever higher force had dealt this unjust hand was capricious and immensely cruel.

Scorching tears stung Landry's eyes.

His mother's delicate features, ashen in contrast to

the pale lavender pillows she rested upon, blurred before his gaze. Summoning gritty determination, he blinked the stinging moisture away, lest Mama witness his grief and become even more distraught.

This dear woman's unconditional love was what had kept him from becoming a replica of the former earl: harsh, unforgiving, selfish, and an abusive, sodding blackguard.

Some claimed giving one's life for another was the greatest gift, and Landry supposed it was. But loving someone unconditionally, even when it guaranteed you'd suffer at another's hands because of that love…

Well, that made his mother a bloody saint in his mind.

Landry had not shed a tear or felt the minutest flicker of grief when his father had kicked off his mortal coil in a most befitting manner—an apoplexy while shagging a Covent Garden doxy.

In truth, it was a wonder the previous earl had not perished from the clap or pox decades ago. It was no more than he deserved.

However, the inflexible, unrelenting reality of never seeing his beloved mother again nearly eviscerated Landry.

God, he screamed silently. Desperately. Futilely.

"Landry, I must…tell you something," Mama

whispered, her voice the merest whisper of sound. An old woman's weak, quavery voice. Not his mother's dulcet tones.

"Shh, Mama," he soothed, leaning down to press his mouth to her too-cool, pale-as-milk forehead. "Save your strength."

It would not be long now.

He swallowed the grief strangling him.

Soon his sweet mother would draw her last labored breath.

Doctor Rendle had left an hour ago. Shaking his silvery-white head, he'd patted Landry's shoulder in a fatherly fashion.

"I am deeply sorry, my lord. There is nothing more to be done. The countess will pass shortly. I have given her laudanum to keep her comfortable."

Rage burgeoned in Landry's chest at the unfairness. *By God in heaven.*

Evil people should die young.

Those as decent and loving as his mother should live to a ripe old age. To see their son married and to hold their grandchildren in their loving embrace. To enjoy the peace and happiness that was denied them for far, *far* too long.

The muffled weeping of Warner, his mother's lady's maid for the past two decades, came from the corner she miserably huddled in. The sniffling and watery shudders agitated Landry, but he did not have the heart to order her to leave the bedchamber.

He well knew how much Warner loved his mother. How, she too, had willingly acted as a buffer between the dying countess and the previous earl's violent rages and calculated cruelty.

"No, Landry. You *must*…listen to me."

Mama grasped his waistcoat, weakly urging him nearer. "I should have told you long ago. Certainly after Keyworth died."

Landry had removed his cravat and coat before the doctor left. It somehow seemed wrong to be attired in starchy formality at a time like this. Besides, the bedchamber was a blistering inferno, the scarlet and orange flames in the hearth fiercely battling each other for dominance in a skirmish neither would win.

Sweat trickled down his back and soaked his underarms. *His* discomfort did not matter. He'd endure hell's fires if it meant easing Mama's suffering a single jot.

Landry forced a smile, though his facial muscles protested the effort, and a merciless vice crushed his breastbone, threatening to pulverize it into dust.

"What is it?" he asked, wishing she would save her strength. Each additional minute with her was a treasure he could store up in his heart and memory.

"You have a sister," Mama whispered through blue-tinted lips.

A sister?

Blinking, he gave his head a sharp shake.

What?

"What?" Landry drew back, his befuddled mind trying to comprehend what she had murmured.

Was she delusional?

Hallucinating?

Was that a sign of impending death?

Pressing two fingers to his temple, he searched the recesses of his mind.

Had Dr. Rendle mentioned anything of that nature possibly occurring as a person died?

Landry honestly did not know.

He could not remember half of what the kindly doctor had told him.

Grief had turned Landry's mind into a foggy, cottony, befuddled mess.

"I named her Lenora, Landry," Mama sobbed softly, a sodden handkerchief pressed to her mouth. "Keyworth was *not* her father."

So his gentle-hearted mother had taken a lover.

Brava for her.

She certainly deserved a sliver of happiness after

having been married to the monster she had called husband for four-and-twenty years. Regardless, his sire's hypocrisy was beyond maddening and equally infuriating.

Where was this sister?

Shunted off to live in obscurity with a distant relative?

Squeezing her hand, he said, "It is all right, Mama."

For what else did one say to one's dying parent when they were confessing their darkest secret?

"He…he did not even permit me to hold her," she muttered raggedly, almost as if speaking to herself. Repeating a phrase she had no doubt murmured over and over and over again to herself in her sorrow.

"She would be ten years old now, my precious little girl," Mama said.

Scorching wrath tunneled through Landry's veins in the next heartbeat. He fought to keep the anger from showing on his face or manifesting in his voice.

He knew of three boys born on the wrong side of the blanket his father had sired—all by different women. And all of whom had been servants in the debaucher's employ.

Undoubtedly, more of the sod's seed had found fertile soil in the countless other women, from the filthiest slatterns to the nobles' perfumed and powdered wives he'd swived. Worse than a rutting bull, the previous earl had not been the least selective or discreet in whom he tupped.

In his typical callous fashion, the reprobate had dismissed his pregnant servants on the grounds of promiscuousness. Likely as not, the bugger had forced himself on them.

When Landry became the earl, he had hired Dirby Madagan, a detective, to locate each ill-used woman and had settled a generous portion on those women and their sons.

It was the least he could do.

And yet…it still was not nearly enough for the disgrace and humiliation the poor misused women had endured. Would continue to endure, for the status of illegitimacy would forever hang over his half-brothers' heads.

Landry had seen to it that the boys received an education, and when they were of an age, he would help them in the vocation of their choice.

How it must've enraged his father to have sired three more sons that he could never claim, while his wife had never born him another child. Just the one heir. Landry. No spare to satisfy the old earl's ego or guarantee the continuance of his spindly, unworthy branch of the family.

Reeling from his mother's confession, Landry asked, "Who is her father?"

All this time, he'd had a sister thirteen years younger than he.

Did she have quicksilver gray eyes and chestnut hair with reddish-bronze ribbons like their mother and him?

Did she possess the same sweet disposition and innocent beauty as their mother?

With apparent effort, his mother tipped her mouth upward a fraction.

"It does not matter, darling. He was not a nobleman or even landed gentry. He died…some time ago. Your father—"

Landry's mother winced, an expression of indescribable anguish flickering across her ravaged features. She licked her chapped lips. "He…"

"Yes?" Landry prompted. "He…?"

"Keyworth…killed him when he learned I was…with child."

"A *duel*?" Landry asked incredulously, unable to disguise his astonishment.

His father had never seemed the honorable or courageous sort.

"No. Keyworth…he shot him in the back." A single crystalline tear trailed from the corner of one eye. "Keyworth gloated about it to me."

She had never called the late earl anything but Keyworth in a carefully neutral tone. As if she had retreated to someplace within herself where he could not hurt her anymore. As if inflecting any emotion into the word validated the monster in some manner.

"He delighted in telling me…all of the horrific details," she whispered brokenly. "How much my darling suffered."

The bloody, bloody murdering blackguard.

"I welcome death." A soft, faraway look entered her gray eyes. "I shall see my beloved again, at last."

"Do you have any idea where the earl would've sent the babe?" Landry asked, now desperate to gather as many details as he could so he could find Lenora. His sister.

Where did Landry start looking, for God's sake?

Ten years was a very long time—*too long?*—to attempt to find a trail likely gone arctic cold.

Nonetheless, he must try.

Mama gave a shallow nod.

"Warner spied on Keyworth for me. He sent Lenora

to live with a family in France. In the *Touraine* region. All of these years, I have tried to find her, but Lenora seemingly disappeared without a trace."

Her voice cracked, and the torment on her frail face ripped Landry's heart from his chest. Another tear trickled from the corner of her eye.

That devil's spawn had sent an innocent babe to live in France while England and France had been at war? He'd probably hoped the child would die.

Or…had *he* disposed of the innocent babe?

Jesus.

That possibility soured Landry's stomach. Bile seared the back of his throat, and acrid bitterness flooded his mouth.

He abhorred the notion—couldn't conceive such evilness.

Regardless of how repulsive the thought, he must consider the possibility. If his sire could cold-bloodedly shoot a man in the back and confiscate a babe at birth, he could also dispose of a defenseless infant without a qualm.

"The physician said I would bear no more children after Lenora. I laughed in Keyworth's face and told him I would cuckold him with any willing man hereafter."

Mama coughed, her thin shoulders quaking.

Landry offered her a drink of water. After a small sip, his mother curved her mouth into a sardonic smile he'd never before seen upon her face.

"It drove him positively mad, trying to figure out who I had been with. There wasn't anyone, of course. Not after…" Her lower lip quivered. "But I so despised him that I made it appear as if there were dozens and dozens."

"Heav'n has no rage, like love to hatred turned, nor hell fury, like a woman scorned."

A rather infamous line from playwright William Congreve whispered across Landry's mind.

How greatly he had underestimated his mother's strength and determination.

She focused her failing gaze across the room.

"It was not hard to do, you know. Keyworth always wanted to believe the worst of me."

Aye, that festering sod's perception of everyone and everything was tinged with his pessimism and his own depraved outlook.

Mama clutched at Landry's hand, suddenly frantic.

"Find her for me, Landry. She should be…with her brother."

She gasped, struggling to breathe for a pair of heartbeats.

A rusty blade skewering his heart would hurt less than watching her suffer—watching her die.

"Promise…me...my son," she rasped, her breathing ever more labored. "Before all else, please make finding your sister your priority." She drew in a shallow, rattling breath. "Then I can…rest in peace, knowing my children have each other."

Holding both of her hands in his, choking on the bevy of sobs throttling up his throat, Landry nodded. His tears flowed freely now, and he did not give a blacksmith's oath. The person he adored the most, his constant in an uncertain and often cruel world, was leaving him.

Forever.

At three-and-twenty, he would be alone.

He had no one.

Except for a ten-year-old sister *somewhere.*

And the possibility of a wife and children someday.

For his own sake, because of what his mother had longed for and been denied, and to spite the rotter burning in hell who'd sired him, Landry would not have a cold, distant marriage filled with icy disdain or fulminating anger.

By God, I would marry a flower hawker or a seamstress if she loved me, and I loved her.

"I shall find her, Mama." He pressed his lips to her icy knuckles.

"Thank you," she uttered so softly that the sound barely slipped past her dry lips.

"I vow it," he swore. "I shall make finding Lenora my top priority."

She was gone before he finished his oath.

1

A windy spring morning
Mayfair, London
3 April 1818

From across the street, Celestia Tolman covertly studied the regal yet unpretentious townhome owned by one of the *haut ton's* most eligible and enigmatic lords. As usual, the morning breeze carried the pungent tang of the River Thames and acrid coal dust.

She wrinkled her nose.

Not a pleasant combination by any means.

Folding her arms in what she hoped was a casual boyish stance, she leaned a shoulder against a plane tree. Bushy tail swishing a warning, a red squirrel scolded her from high upon its lofty perch.

Wouldn't Mama be horrified to see her usually

prim and proper daughter thus attired and bent on an escapade that was at best imprudent?

At worst…

No. NO, Celestia admonished herself more strenuously.

She would not dwell on the many, *many* disagreeable possibilities.

Besides, she had done her research and had memorized the layout of the building's five stories, not counting the attic space. Acquiring the house's blueprints and the other equally impressive homes marching along the same lane like a row of matching uniformed soldiers had not been difficult.

Records and archives of building plans and blueprints were accessible if one knew where to look. As she worked in a used bookstore, Pattern Books produced by architects and designers were not unfamiliar to her. To be sure, they were not the most titillating of reading, but they were quite informative when one planned on sneaking into a lord's house.

Which she did.

Today.

This day's objective was the study, situated at the rear of the house on the ground floor. A study that opened onto a narrow terrace, facing a not-so-well-tended small garden area. That particular detail was somewhat surprising given what she knew about the uncompromising, inflexible lord who lived there.

She would've thought *he* was the sort of starchy, rigid, self-important peer to have an apoplexy if a single leaf dared fall onto the lush grass. She suspected the monstrous black dog she'd spied a time or two loping about the enclosure might be the reason for the garden's less than pristine condition.

Probably a watchdog trained to rip trespassers to pieces.

She shivered and ducked her neck lower into the scarf tied there.

Pray God that shaggy, colt-sized brute was not wandering the corridors unattended today. The creature was quite the largest dog she had ever seen.

Regardless, the garden was another escape route if her encounter with Landry Audsley, Earl of Keyworth, went sideways. Or to Hades in the devil's knitting basket, as Mama used to say. Which, on further consideration, really made no sense at all.

What need would the devil have for knitted anything?

Hell was blazing hot, after all. Besides, wouldn't Lucifer be far too busy wreaking havoc on peoples' lives to bother with natty spinsters' hobby?

Huddled into a moth-eaten, charcoal-gray twill

coat—one of her brother Nash's discards from a decade ago—Celestia directed her attention to the pavement whenever anyone passed by on foot, atop a horse, or in a conveyance.

It was best to appear bashful and inconspicuous—no more noticeable than the bark on the tree supporting her at present. For good measure and to give the impression of a woebegone street urchin, she had even smudged soot on her cheeks, nose, forehead, and chin.

Mama would roll over in her grave if she could see what drastic, unladylike measures Celestia had stooped to.

And Papa?

Well, he'd suffer a paroxysm for sure.

Uncle Paul would laugh heartily, though, thinking it great, good fun, as would Nash and Orion.

Nonetheless, Celestia's nerves were strung taut as the proverbial bowstring. Trepidation for what she was about to do had left her mouth as dry as the toast she had tried—*unsuccessfully*—to eat for breakfast almost four hours ago. Even after spreading strawberry preserves on the triangle, she'd only managed one bite.

At this moment, she was hard-pressed to produce a single drop of moisture in her mouth.

Celestia blew on her cold fingers before rubbing her

ungloved hands together. Her gloves were far too feminine to pass muster for a delivery boy's. Papa's and Uncle Paul's were too large, and her brothers' boyhood gloves all seemed to be missing their mates.

A rare grin swept her face for a second.

As children, Orion and Nash were forever losing their gloves. After a slight scold—Mama could never remain vexed with any of her children for long—she would knit them a new pair with whatever shade of yarn she possessed the most of.

As quickly as it had appeared, Celestia's humor faded, and a dull ache gripped her heart.

She missed her rambunctious, teasing older brothers.

Mama too. Unbearably so at times.

Times like these when Celestia was forced to act as the head of the family and make impossible decisions that would impact them all, for better or worse.

The squirrel began a new scold, this one somewhat agitated.

Celestia glanced upward and spied a crow perched on a branch, head cocked and eyeing her with its tiny, unnerving black eyes.

Well, that couldn't be a good omen.

Giving herself a mental shake, Celestia resumed her perusal of the townhome. It was much too late for second thoughts. She had already put her well-thought-out plan in motion.

A small cloth bag containing a sugar cone with precious, expensive white sugar was tucked inside her coat pocket. The sugar was her means of entering Keyworth's home as a delivery lad.

My key to Keyworth's.

She chuckled to herself at the awful jest.

Paradoxically, though the wind was biting under a few scattered, slumberous pale gray clouds, anxiety-borne sweat trickled in sticky rivulets down her back and dampened her underarms and hands in a cruel juxtaposition of cold and hot.

Icy dread and smoldering anger.

Swiping her moist palms against the front of the woolen jacket, Celestia dried her hands, then balled them into tight fists. Her rounded nails cut crescents into the soft flesh, yet she welcomed the sting.

The pain kept Celestia focused and reminded her of her purpose.

Why she was here.

What—*who*—had brought her to this desperate

position.

Landry Audsley, the contemptible, irascible, *unreasonable* Earl of Keyworth.

If Celestia were a man, she would call out the black-hearted bounder living in luxury across the street for sullying the Tolmans' heretofore good name and nearly destroying their business. Too bad she was not of a vengeful bent, else she would spread nasty rumors about him and ruin *his* reputation as he had done to the Tolmans.

More specifically, Tolman Tomes—Scrivener and Stationer.

Instead, she had to rely upon her wit, intelligence, and a good deal of luck, truth to tell, to accomplish her purpose. A little favor and grace from the Almighty would not be amiss either. Although, asking for the Lord's help and protection when she intended to illicitly enter a peer's home seemed the quintessence of irreverent hypocrisy.

Two lanky men conversing animatedly in thick Cockney accents approached, and she pointed her gaze toward her scuffed boots into which she had tucked her several inches too long trousers.

Thank goodness Nash had been a chubby youth, or

else Celestia never would've been able to pull his old black trousers over her rounded hips. A length of wide blue ribbon served as a belt to secure the gaping waist. Beneath her borrowed coat, her breasts strained against the lawn shirt—one of Orion's outgrown garments.

Sentimentality had prevented her from disposing of the trunks of old clothing and other assorted items no longer of use and stored in the attic of the house she shared with Papa and Uncle Paul. Situated in an older but still quite respectable neighborhood, the house was similar to dozens of others in the area: unremarkable but comfortable.

Celestia had what Mama called a *voluptuous* figure. In other words, her womanly curves were indeed *very* apparent and more than once had drawn unsolicited masculine attention.

Most often, not for honorable reasons either.

Last week, while she had been arranging the new inventory of cheroots and cigars in the display at Tolman Tomes—Scrivener and Stationer, a pudgy dandy, smelling of mutton and violet water of all things, had cornered her. *Again.*

Vowing undying devotion, Ignatius Cronk—the third son of Viscount Ballew— had for the fourth time—*or was it the fifth?*—beseeched Celestia to allow him to become her protector.

He was the seventh degenerated codpate to insult her with such a vulgar offer and then dared to act affronted when she coldly, possibly rather rudely, refused his offensive proposition.

Men. Tosspots all.

No, not so.

Nash and Orion were not like those men—libertines and bounders. Neither were Papa nor Uncle Paul. Her father and his older brother had adored their wives—still did, though Mama had been gone these three years past and Aunt Rosalie eight years now.

Celestia curved her mouth into a droll, derisive smile.

She was an unapologetically prim bluestocking who chose to wear drab, shapeless gowns to discourage male attention. Gowns in muted, unflattering shades and boasting such high necklines that a nun would envy the modest garments.

Celestia typically twisted her ordinary brown hair into a sensible, tight knot too. What was more, she also usually possessed ink-stained fingers, a clear testament to her lowly station.

Nevertheless, according to Mr. Cronk, she was an, *"irresistible temptress. A goddess of unparalleled beauty and form."*

She rolled her eyes skyward at the nauseating memory of him waxing poetic. Her jaundiced view of society was well-earned, nevertheless.

That vile Mr. Cronk had licked his protruding froggy lips and boldly ogled her generous bosom, though it was covered by an apron and her slate-gray gown. He behaved as if he were doing her the greatest honor by asking her to become his paramour.

Could he really be so dull-witted?

"My dear, dear, Celestia. A woman of *your* station," Cronk wheedled, dragging the *your* out and making the word three syllables, "cannot expect anything more from an individual so superior to you in station and birth."

How easily the nobility trespassed.

That baconbrain had actually had the ballocks to say that to her. It had taken all of Celestia's self-control not to stab his lordship with one of the nearby metal quill nibs or crack him atop the head with a very thick book.

Was she supposed to be grateful that he, along with

the others, had offered her money, jewels, and gewgaws for her ruination? Her virtue? The loss of her self-respect? Degradation and disgrace?

Yes. Yes, indeed she was.

The lower orders were always expected to worship the hallowed ground aristocrats trod upon. Never mind that birth, position, or titles did not in any way make one superior in character or moral fabric.

True, Celestia's lineage boasted a noble peer or three on various distant and gnarled Tolman family tree branches. Mama had also been the great-granddaughter of a viscount.

However, Celestia, like her brothers and their father before them, were of the working class. *They* smelled of the shop, which to *le beau monde* was akin to ailing from a highly contagious and deadly disease.

Better to smell of the shop than mutton and violet water.

It had been Nash's idea to begin selling quality tobacco products. Snuff, cheroots, pipe tobacco, pipes and the like—only the most sought-after items preferred by the gentry and aristocrats.

Tobacco was popular with the upper ten thousand, and he reasoned they would venture into the shop and, while they were there, purchase a book or stationery items. Or, perhaps, even hire a scrivener.

Regrettably, the latter had not occurred.

No new clients had sought scribe or transcribing services in weeks. Not since Lord Hard-hearted Keyworth had discharged Papa. The likelihood that the simultaneous decline in the shop's business and Papa's dismissal was a coincidence was as implausible as Celestia becoming a lady.

That would never happen. Not only due to her lowly birth but because, unlike many feather-brained young women, the idea was as abhorrent as a leprosy diagnosis.

Firming her mouth against the shiver scuttling from her waist to her shoulders, she hunched further into her coat, pulling the collar higher against the annoyingly brisk wind.

The oversized garment hung to her knees, disguising her feminine curves. She felt confident her nondescript clothing, perfect for a humble delivery boy, would not draw attention nor reveal her gender.

She had plaited her waist-length hair and tucked the thick rope into a knitted cap pulled low on her forehead—another discarded item of one of her brothers. For good measure, she wore a shabby muffler around her neck, half-covering her lower face. Not much other than her eyes, cheeks, and nose were visible.

Celestia sucked her lower lip between her teeth. Mindful of the immense risk she was about to undertake, she reviewed her methodically and meticulously crafted plan.

This must work.

It had to.

Too much was at stake if she were not successful.

Aye, however, a gossamer-thin thread divided boldness from folly.

This is foolhardiness at its absolute worst, Celestia Andromeda Josette Tolman. If you are caught...

2

*I apologize, your lordship, but that lead in
Devonshire has resulted in another dead end.
No one I spoke with there has ever heard of
anyone named Smythe-Shufflebottom.
How should I proceed?*

*~Letter to Landry Audsley, Earl of Keyworth, from
Dirby Madagan, investigator*

*Keyworth House
Mayfair, London
That Same April Morning*

*G*od's wounds.

Another deuced dead end.

For eight interminable years, Landry had been searching for his sister. Eight years of dead ends, false leads, impasses, and so much blasted frustration.

Well, not entirely.

After Mama's death, he had toddled off to the continent to search for his sister and learned that his despicable father had not sent Lenora to France after all. That had simply been a ruse the blackguard had contrived to put Warner off the trail. The cur had known the maid was eavesdropping and would relay the false information to the distraught countess.

What an unmitigated whoremonger to deliberately deceive his wife. Landry's father had known Mama would search for her daughter, and the old earl had ensured she would never find Lenora.

May his black soul burn in the ninth level of hell.

It had taken Madagan months, but he had been able to trace the wet nurse hired to care for Landry's sister as well as the coachman who had driven the coach that night. Each vowed the babe had been left with a childless vicar, Reverend Cornelius Smythe-Shufflebottom, and his wife in Lancaster.

Four years later, the vicar had died after falling down the parish church steps and hitting his head. Local tattle suggested it mightn't have been an accident. If rumors were to be believed—there was generally a nugget of truth buried within gossip if one dug deep enough—the vicar was not exactly the model of piety and virtue.

After his *accident*, his widow, along with Lenora, appeared to have disappeared off the face of the earth. No one knew where they had gone. Neither did anyone know a blasted thing about the deceased vicar's or his elusive wife's family.

How could a parish be so ill-informed about their cleric?

According to the letter Landry held, the reverend had not been precisely beloved by his congregation. Reverend Smythe-Shufflebottom had been coldly aloof, arrogantly judgmental, and severely critical, which accounted for the sparse attendance to hear his gloom and doom sermons every Sunday.

As Landry stood before the French windows leading to the gardens, he assessed the grounds with a critical eye. He absently patted Sampson's oversized head. The dog leaned into his leg, all ten stones of him, and Landry had to brace his stance against the Newfoundland's weight.

Sampson had absolutely no concept of his size and occasionally still tried to crawl onto Landry's lap.

He probably ought to hire a real gardener to tend the area rather than the lads from the streets. But truth be told, the urchins needed the blunt more. If that meant his flower beds, hedgerows, and grass failed to measure up to the *ton's* haughty approval, he did not give a beggar's curse.

The *haut ton's* approval didn't put food in starving children's bellies.

He also employed street youths in his townhome, except for the kitchen.

Jolly of disposition and with a ready smile upon her face, Mrs. Cox had stood her ground when it came to the kitchen's cleanliness. She had even threatened Landry with a rolling pin. And as he adored her pastries, biscuits, and other treats, he was not about to alienate his talented cook.

Furthermore, Landry did not retain a housekeeper. Not for want of trying, however.

Seven housekeepers had given notice and hightailed it within a week when he'd informed the women their duties included training homeless girls as maids. Every single housekeeper believed it beneath her to provide the waifs with a means to earn a respectable living. Even paying the prideful women an exorbitant salary had not persuaded them to stay on.

In the end, Landry had given up on retaining a proper housekeeper.

Instead, one of his long-time parlor maids—herself a former street rat—had agreed to take on the task. Hence, there might be half a dozen or so girls and boys ranging in age from seven to seventeen on the premises performing all manner of chores on any given day.

They would leave with a full belly, often a new article of clothing, and much-needed coin.

When he could, Landry placed the younger children in various foundling homes run by his philanthropic friends. There were not nearly enough beds available, however. A better solution would be to build institutions that provided the children a place to live, education, and vocational training.

Many of the upper class thought those ideas dangerously radical, and those who adopted that viewpoint wanted no part in funding such establishments. Ironically, those same pompous peers grumbled incessantly about the multitude of pickpockets and other street rabble.

How, pray tell, did the *haut ton* expect the children to keep from starving?

Did they have any idea how many of those unfortunate urchins did indeed starve?

No, and most of the upper class did not want to know.

Ignorance being bliss and all of that tripe.

Cupping his nape, Landry perused the letter from the investigator he had retained all those years ago to locate his illegitimate brothers for the third time.

How should I proceed? Madagan asked.

Indeed, how *should* he?

Landry glanced at his dog, acquired soon after his mother died to offset his unbearable loneliness.

"How should we proceed, Sampson?"

Sampson gave him a doggy smile and thumped his massive tail.

"Just so."

Landry scratched behind the dog's ears. A bit of drool hung from his mouth—not an uncommon occurrence.

"I shan't give up, Sampson. Lenora's out there somewhere, and I mean to find her."

Mayhap…yes, indeed, mayhap it *was* time to hire a new investigator.

But who?

At one time, Mathias Pembroke, Duke of Westfall, had been an amateur sleuth. He might know of someone qualified. Someone younger and perhaps with a bit more prowess and ambition than the aging and less than motivated Dirby Madagan.

Landry had suspected for some time that Madagan was not up to the task any longer.

Perchance, one of the earls at the Wicked Earls' Club might be able to recommend someone. That lot was neckcloth deep in mischief half of the time. All right, *most* of the time. Undoubtedly one of the earls could point him in the right direction.

Rubbing his chin, Landry mentally ran through the most likely candidates to be of assistance.

Baxter? Sharonford? Kendal? Alnwick? Brecken?

Assuredly *not* Mosely or Harrison. Or Thuxby, for that matter.

When not foxed or whoring, the former were always stirring up trouble in the House of Lords. They did not appreciate advancement, nor did they like anyone who advocated for change. By no means was Landry a Whig, but common decency demanded everyone with positions of power aid those less fortunate than themselves.

And not by giving them handouts over and over again.

As the proverb went, "Give a man a fish, and you feed him for a day; teach a man to fish, and you feed him for a lifetime."

Thuxby was simply a pompous windbag who abhorred any type of forward-thinking and would do most anything to squash what he termed "*dangerous, rebellious, insurrectionist ideologies.*"

In truth, the prime minister, Lord Liverpool, was

cut from much the same narrow-minded cloth as Thuxby. Stuffy, stuck-in-a-rut, mule-headed bores, both.

Except, whereas Landry believed Lord Liverpool genuinely wanted what was best for England, Thuxby's motives were purely self-serving.

Rumors abounded about the man's deviant preferences as well.

Regrettably, Landry's principles and philosophies were not echoed by the majority of the lords. George Tierney, the House of Commons leader, was a jot more amenable, but Landry needed the lords' support for what he had in mind.

At that rumination, he grimaced.

He had a speech to write, and it was not going to pen itself as much as he wished otherwise. He'd terminated his increasingly incompetent scribe a few months ago. Now Landry was obliged to write his own speeches, rather than dictating them as had been his habit and, truth to tell, was still his preference.

Competent, entirely trustworthy, and loyal scribes were not easily come by.

Blasted impossible to find, in point of fact.

Writing, principally spelling and grammar, were

not tasks Landry particularly excelled at. He meant to have Baxter and Sharonford review the entire speech—word for word—before his presentation in Parliament lest he make a laughingstock of himself.

Too blasted bad, Jonathan Tolman had bumbled so drastically that Landry could not risk using the scrivener any longer after six years. The amanuensis had inadvertently delivered the third chapter of *A Mistress's Memoirs: The Daily Duties of a Demimonde* to Landry and had, presumably, delivered Landry's speech to the courtesan.

Mouth turned downward, he shook his head.

God only knew what the lady of the evening had done with his work.

Probably tossed his presentation into the fire as he had been tempted to do with her, ah…borderline erotic musings. For certain, Madame Meriette Bonacieux—assuredly not her real name—had not returned the papers to him.

Which had meant, blast it all, Landry had no choice but to rewrite the deuced thing again himself.

His reproachful speech on society's responsibility to the homeless children populating London's streets and how he regularly assisted them was far less scintillating or titillating than the paramour's sexual escapades with several well-known aristocrats.

Chapter three made reference to two lords with whom Landry was pretty confident he was acquainted. Surely Lenkershire was none other than Lord George-Walter Lankershim and Ferndale must be Lord Wendell Fawndale.

The meagerest alteration of her clients' names suggested Meriette Bonacieux had a rancorous streak and wanted her former protectors to squirm.

A sideways grin pulled Landry's mouth up on one side.

He had not believed Lankershim physically capable of the maneuvers Madame Bonacieux described in embarrassing, rather repugnant detail, given Lankershim's turnip-shape form. Lady Lankershim mightn't be overly thrilled her libertine husband was named in the courtesan's memoir either.

Landry had half a mind to purchase the book just to see who else Madame Bonacieux publicly outed.

Upon further reflection, he grimaced, turning his mouth downward.

Nay, perhaps not.

He would not be able to look any of those men in

the eye again and not see what she had so vividly described and either smirk or laugh outright as in Lankershim's case.

Some things could not be erased from one's mind or imagination.

Of equal concern was that Tolman had not even brought the transcribed documents to Landry himself— a term Landry had insisted upon for privacy reasons.

Instead, Tolman had sent the confidential documents with a delivery boy. A lad hired straight off the street. The risk of a Whig or someone with a more nefarious intention getting their hands on Landry's speech before he could present his case to Parliament was inexcusable.

Landry had, in fact, returned Madame Bonacieux's packet to Jonathan Tolman the day the man had come to entreat Landry to reconsider his dismissal. However, Tolman had arrived smelling strongly of spirits and slurring his words.

Any inclination Landry might've had for clemency promptly flew straight out the window—which he had been compelled to open in January, so pungent was the aroma of liquor on Tolman—when the scribe hiccupped and dragged a flask from his pocket.

Landry could not risk dictating delicate subject matter to a drunkard.

Pulling himself from his reverie, he sighed.

"Let's be about it, Sampson. If I finish in time, I shall take you for a long walk in Green Park. How does that sound?"

The only thing Sampson loved more was racing across the meadows at Faringcroft Park.

Sampson gave a little woof of approval, and drool dripped onto the carpet.

Landry grabbed the linen left for just such a purpose, bent, and wiped up the mess.

Sampson took the opportunity to lick his cheek.

"Yes, I love you too, you great brute. Now go lay down while I attempt to wrestle a speech from yonder quill, and do try not to drool all over everything."

A fool's hope, that.

Sampson obediently wandered to the fireplace and, after circling precisely five times—never four or six—with a loud *oomph*, plopped his large, furry body down. His ebony muzzle resting on his big paws, he watched Landry's every move with soulful brown eyes.

Landry glanced to the burr walnut drumhead mantel clock.

Three hours to work on his speech, an hour in the park with Sampson, and then on to the Wicked Earls' Club. Hopefully, though it would be fairly early in the day, one of his friends would be around to consult about an investigator.

While he was out and about, Landry intended to place an advert for an amanuensis. He might as well since his days of oration in Parliament were over unless he could memorize his speeches. And most inconveniently, he would still have to write the bloody things first to do that.

"Damn," he cursed beneath his breath as he settled into the chair.

It crackled softly as worn leather is wont to do. Clearing his thoughts of Lenora for the time being, he bent his head and set to the task of convincing the House of Lords that it was their civic duty as well as common Christian decency to aid the homeless waifs.

What if...

A most unwelcome thought penetrated his concentration, causing him to pause mid-word.

Landry shook his head to dispel the ugly idea.

Nevertheless, the deuced persistent notion would not go away.

What if Lenora and her adopted mother did not have anywhere to go after the vicar passed?

What if…

What if Lenora *was* living on the streets?

Or worse?

She had been forced into prostitution to survive?

Fiend seize it.

His gut wrenched sickeningly.

He pulled out a clean sheet of foolscap. Another much more pressing matter than his speech required his attention. He'd send a note round to Sharonford and ask the earl to meet him at The Wicked Earls' Club.

Landry must hire a new detective as soon as possible.

3

What if I am compromised? Arrested? Or...worse?
What becomes of Papa and Uncle then?
But what other recourse have I?
Our situation has become truly dire.

~Miss Celestia Tolman to her diary

Across the Street from Keyworth House
Mayfair, London
3 April 1818 – Still Morning

If Celestia was caught, well, at least she would have done her utmost to save her father's reputation and that of Tolman Tomes—Scrivener and Stationer too. Since January, the requests for note-taking and transcribing had trickled to nearly nothing when the Earl of Keyworth had dismissed Papa as his amanuensis.

For the past several weeks, only the scarcely sufficient sales of used books and tobacco and stationery supplies had kept the shop operating. For decades, the bulk of the establishment's income had come from the professional, confidential, and estimable scrivener and scribe services provided by the Tolman brothers.

And me.

That included taking shorthand and then translating the notes for dictated books, contracts, other documents, all nature of research, and even long-winded, *boring* speeches for members of Parliament.

The odious Earl of Keyworth had obviously blabbed to his elite cronies about Papa's single unfortunate disgrace.

Why else would the shop's loyal clientele have dwindled so drastically and so swiftly?

No, Keyworth must be spreading incendiary tales.

A scalding swell of anger blunted Celestia's apprehension, and she squared her shoulders in rebellion as she pulled her mouth into a mutinous line.

Keyworth had forced her into taking drastic measures.

Hadn't she tried all of the reasonable and respectable avenues to speak with him?

Of course, she had.

What prudent woman wouldn't have done?

A contemptuous snort escaped her, earning her an odd look from a thin-faced, red-cheeked woman bustling past in a too-thin cloak.

Celestia had politely requested an audience with the earl.

Multiple times, in truth.

She had written at least a score of carefully worded letters over the past three months. More if she counted the notes she had thrown away after her dratted temper had taken hold of her.

Those times, she had told the unmerciful, condemning, arrogant blackguard precisely what she thought of him in the most indelicate of terms. Terms a prim and proper young lady had no business knowing, but that also came with working in a used bookstore. There was a ready supply of reading material, and no one had ever thought to censor her choices.

What was more, she had also called at his lordship's residence no less than eight times.

Eight blasted times.

And on each and *every* occasion, a monstrous butler, who appeared from his battered face to have been a prizefighter in his youth, had turned her away with a frosty frown and thin-lipped disdain.

Had the great brute even told the earl she had called? A single time?

Or—she scowled darkly as a thought sprang to mind—had Keyworth given a standing order that *all* Tolmans were to be turned away?

Likely the latter, the unfeeling fiend.

Papa had given up speaking to the earl after one evidently very unpleasant attempt to regain favor with his lordship. He'd come home that January afternoon and drunk himself into a tippler's stupor. Not an uncommon occurrence since Mama's death, and if Celestia were wholly honest, the reason they were in this shamble to begin with too.

Papa really must sober up, or all might be lost, even if the earl agreed to rehire him.

She was at her wit's end with her father, and compassion and sympathy had gravitated into frustration and resentment. Which, in turn, made her feel guilty and like the worst sort of wretched daughter.

Celestia shifted her position to better view the alley running between the two grand homes, and though she wore three pairs of her father's thick socks, her feet slipped slightly in the too-big boots. The narrow, cobbled lane leading to the mews and coach houses behind the grand homes was most conveniently used for deliveries to the earl's residence.

After a fortnight of watching the household's routine, she had learned various lads between ten and twelve years old made frequent deliveries. Almost daily, in point of fact, and they always entered through a gate in the rock wall.

The boys descended the stairs to the basement door and knocked three times.

A kindly, round-faced servant admitted them.

The lads left a short while later, usually munching a biscuit, a cinnamon bun, or perhaps a slice of seed cake.

Celestia had spoken to the two boys she had most often seen making the deliveries and convinced one, Petey, to aide her.

Today was sugar delivery day.

The earl, it seemed, had quite a sweet tooth. Probably needed all of that sugar to offset his sour disposition and acerbic temperament.

She had paid Petey, the sugar delivery boy, five pounds—a veritable fortune to a street lad—to allow her to make today's delivery in his stead. After that, Petey had been an absolute fountain of information, explaining that the earl always requested the merchants use ragamuffins and street urchins to make the deliveries rather than the merchant's own employees.

Celestia considered that rather odd.

Wouldn't the merchant's delivery boys be more

trustworthy?

She gave a mental shrug.

But what did she know of such matters?

Petey's eyes shone with admiration, and a grin wreathed his thin face when he spoke of the earl. As she assuredly did not share his esteem of his lordship, Celestia had remained silent as Petey extolled Keyworth's many praiseworthy virtues.

"He don' let the merchants deliver everythin' at once like most swells do." Petey had leaned in and winked. "The earl wants more of the boys to have a chance to make a few coins. He's a big tipper, he is. 'Specially if he's pleased with ya."

As Celestia shopped for her household, she had no notion of what was typical for the *haut ton,* nor did she really care. Regardless, she could not conceive this benevolent, saintlike version of the Earl of Keyworth that Petey described.

"The earl's butler, Teeven, is a right scary chap. Grunts more than talks most of the time. But yer in luck." His dirt-smudged, freckled face alight with importance, Petey grinned, revealing slightly crooked teeth. "Friday mornin's are Teeven's half-day off."

He scratched his towhead. Vigorously.

Lice?

"Queer that," Petey said with a final enthusiastic scrape across his scalp with dirty, jagged fingernails. "Most butlers have Sundays off."

How he'd come by that tidbit, Celestia could not imagine.

A petulant gust of wind tried to whip her cap from her head, and she slapped a palm to her scalp to keep it in place. It might be April, but spring had yet to reveal herself. Winter's chill lingered in the air.

Celestia shivered, though whether from the dank breeze or the tension thrumming through her, she did not know. How she yearned for her warm pelisse or cloak to bundle around herself as a buffer against the persistent wind. Instead, she wrapped herself in determination and tenacity. There was no one else to resolve this *misunderstanding* between Papa and the earl.

Keyworth *must* be made to see reason and agree to give Papa another chance.

But Papa *must* also put aside his drink.

Her brothers, Nash and Orion, were off doing whatever sailors in His Majesty's Navy did. They seldom came home anymore, and when they did, they were eager to depart for another adventure when their leave ended.

Her brothers had not had to deal with their father's melancholy and increased drinking after Mama's death either. Nor his decline into the doldrums or his incapacitating grief. Neither did they fret nightly about making ends meet or whether the store would remain open another month.

Celestia had taken over transcribing for Papa, although that was a well-guarded secret.

For the past eight years, she had worked closely with him, and he had occasionally allowed her to transcribe the shorthand notes he'd taken into longhand for his patrons. She also knew how to take notes in shorthand and frequently did so while working at the bookstore to save time.

After Mama's passing, Papa had increasingly permitted her to clandestinely transcribe his notes except for those of his most elite patrons, including the Earl of Keyworth.

A swift glance at the timepiece she had tucked into her pocket confirmed what she'd suspected. It was almost nine of the clock.

With a fortifying gulp of air and a prayer sent

heavenward that she would be successful, she darted across the street. Giving a quick glance up and down the alley, she slipped through the gate and descended the short stairwell.

As Petey had told her to, she knocked thrice upon the wood panel.

A few blinks later, the friendly faced, plump cook opened the door. Wiping her hands on a towel, she eyed Celestia curiously.

"Ye're a new laddie, ain't ye?"

"Aye, ma'am." Adopting a street accent, Celestia lowered her voice and kept her gaze riveted on the threshold. "The name's Tom."

A common enough name she'd decided upon, unlike her and her brothers' unusual names.

"Petey sprained his ankle. I came in his stead."

"Poor laddie." The servant's brow pleated like a fan in worry. "I'll tell his lordship. He'll be concerned. He may want to send a physician 'round to look at Pete."

Caught off guard for a fraction, Celestia gaped.

What peer did that?

"Nay. Nay need for that. He's already limpin' about," she said, scrambling for an excuse. She leaned in and whispered, "Betwixt you and me, I think he wanted me to have a chance to earn a bit o' coin. I am a bit down on me luck."

That was not a lie.

"Well, come in, Tom. I have a treacle on the stove that I need to get back to. By the by, I am Mrs. Cox."

With that, the sturdy woman in her black gown and crisp white apron and cap trundled inside. She returned to the stove and stirred the heavenly smelling treacle.

Celestia followed her, noting the neat-as-a-pin kitchen. If a single speck of dust or a crumb had escaped notice, she'd dance a jig. She pulled the sugar cone from her jacket, then withdrew it from the protective bag.

"Where should I put the sugar?"

She held up the blue-and-white papered cylinder.

Mrs. Cox did not look up but angled her head toward a table by an open door leading into a shadowy corridor. Several loaves of bread, Shrewsbury biscuits, and ginger buns cooled upon its spotless surface.

"Help yerself to a biscuit or ginger bun, Tom," she said, leaning over to examine the pot's contents. "His lordship insists upon treatin' his lads well, he does."

Approval laced her voice, as did evident admiration for her employer.

Were all servants and underlings enamored of the

Earl of Keyworth?

Why?

The man was positively beastly.

Celestia seized the moment and slipped into the corridor. Breath held, she rushed along on tiptoe. As she rounded a corner, she heard Mrs. Cox mumble, "Hmph. Bashful, that one. He left without sayin' farewell and without his tip too."

A satisfied grin pulled at the edges of Celestia's mouth as she rushed up the servants' stairway, praying all the while that the gargantuan dog was not inside the house.

4

*Are you available to meet at
The Wicked Earls' Club at half-past two
this afternoon? I require immediate
advice of a delicate nature.*

*~Urgent note to the Earl of Sharonford from the
Earl of Keyworth*

*The Earl of Keyworth's Study
Keyworth House
An Hour Later*

Landry's nape prickled, and he knew he was not alone a blink before Sampson jumped to his feet. The dog swung his head toward the door—a spray of drool flying across the room—and gave a deep, warning woof. Many a grown man quaked in fear when the Newfoundland approached.

Not a servant.

The dog would not have sounded a warning had it been.

"Shh, boy. Stay."

Sampson plopped his haunches onto the floor, but

his attention remained riveted on the other side of the room.

He thumped his ropelike tail thrice.

Not a threat then, either.

Taking his time to settle the quill in its brass holder beside the chariot-shaped inkwell, Landry turned his head and took in the waif standing uncertainly four feet inside his study.

The lad might've been fourteen or fifteen. A little older than the boys that generally made deliveries or brought messages. Likely a waif with younger siblings to feed. And from the nervous glances he kept spearing Sampson, not accustomed to dogs either.

Well, not dogs as large as Sampson, in any event. But to be fair, most people weren't.

Sharonford had responded much quicker than Landry expected his carousing friend to.

He grinned his satisfaction, and a shadow played across the lad's features.

Typically, the earl did not even find his mattress until the wee hours of the morning. For Sharonford to be upright and revived enough to respond to Landry's urgent missive before noon was either exceedingly peculiar, or it meant Sharonford had, at last, turned over a new leaf.

And Sampson dines with a knife and fork.

Or—a third explanation poked its head up.

Sharonford had not been to bed yet.

That, quite plausibly, was the correct explanation.

"Have you a message for me?" Landry asked when the tongue-tied youth continued to hover mere feet from the doorway. As if he heartily yearned to turn tail and run but did not dare. Either because he feared Sampson would attack or was desperate for the coin he hoped to receive by way of a tip for a job well done.

Mrs. Cox or Henrietta, the parlor maid, must've sent the lad along, as Teeven spent Friday mornings with his ailing father.

A faint smile tipped Landry's mouth.

His household was anything but ordinary, to be sure. It was a good thing he had vowed to his mother not to wed until he'd found Lenora. Landry was not at all sure his future countess would appreciate his lax strictures or irregular staff.

At the time—eight years ago, to be precise—that vow had seemed reasonable.

But now…?

Well, he had not yet given up on finding his sister. Neither had he specified he would *not* wed—only that he would make finding his sister his highest priority.

Besides, he was only one-and-thirty. Not quite ready to stick his spoon in the wall or cock up his toes just yet.

Glancing at his speech upon the desk, he pulled his eyebrows together in consternation.

Only three bloody paragraphs?

It felt like he'd labored over those few words for hours. A glance at the mantel clock revealed an hour had indeed passed. Whenever he was deep in thought, time flew by.

If Landry still retained a scrivener, the task would've been completed by now.

When the boy did not answer, he looked up again.

"Come then. Hand it over. I am quite busy."

This speech must be finished by Monday so that his friends might peruse it before he spoke before Parliament.

He extended his hand, eager to see if his friend was available to meet with him later today.

Sampson meandered forward and proceeded to sniff the lad. He snuffled at the boy's scuffed boots, leaving a wet trail across the lad's scruffy footwear, then made a slow circle around the white-faced, rigid youth.

Perhaps the lad was afraid of dogs.

Landry gave a low whistle and, at once, Sampson

padded to his side.

The messenger breathed out a visible breath of relief.

"My message?" Landry repeated, a tad less patiently.

"I do not have a message for you, my lord," came the lad's low reply.

Landry narrowed his eyes and furrowed his brow.

Much, *much* too articulate and refined for a street youth.

Who was he?

Eyebrow cocked, a half-smile bending his mouth, Landry leaned back.

"Then why are you here? Looking for work?"

He supposed his groom and stable hand could use another pair of hands.

Not truly, but they would find something for the boy to earn a few coins: oil the harnesses and the like.

Isn't that what one did to harnesses and saddles?

He felt rather like a pampered idiot that he had absolutely no idea.

Inhaling a deep breath, his fingertips scraping the front of his coat, the youth advanced toward the desk. When he stood directly before Landry, the lad removed his hideous hat, and a long, thick, unassuming brown braid tumbled free.

Zounds.

Not a lad at all but a lovely young lady.

At least Landry thought she was lovely beneath the smudges on her face. Her skin appeared far too creamy, the delicate planes of her face too smooth, and her startling green eyes far too innocent for a street rat, however.

An aristocrat or two must've perched haphazardly in her family tree somewhere. Her fine-boned features were a contradiction of her birth if that were not the case, and he'd be bound it was.

Umbrage glinting in her gaze, now narrowed to jade slits, she unwound the ugly as sin scarf from around her neck.

She was angry. Livid, if Landry had to venture a guess.

But why?

A rosy hue tinged her face beneath a generous sprinkling of freckles.

Anger, nerves, or fear?

Or was she merely too warm from the heavy coat she wore?

Leaning forward, Landry placed his elbows on his desk and steepled his ink-stained fingers. He'd discarded his jacket upon entering the study this morning, and it lay slung across the claret-colored leather divan. As was his habit, he'd rolled his shirtsleeves up his forearms to prevent any chance of getting ink upon them.

Amused reproof made his lips twitch.

He was not a tidy writer as the ink-smudged paper before him attested.

The young woman swiftly perused his study, no doubt taking in every detail, before she settled her gaze disconcertingly on him.

How old was she?

More on point, why was she here?

Landry casually scrutinized the wraith before him. Eyebrows knit together in an elegant line, her eyes shone with silent fervor. She was either exceptionally courageous or extraordinarily imprudent.

Her clothing was of fair quality, appropriate for the merchant class, but years and *years* out of fashion. Her oversized coat hid much of her figure, but well-shaped legs disappeared into boots he'd wager were several sizes too large for her small feet.

"My lord, I am Celestia Tolman of Tolman Tomes—Scrivener and Stationer."

Ah. Now the puzzle came together.

The tenor of her voice, dark warm honey, surrounded Landry: husky, lyrical, and very, *very* feminine. How could he have not realized she was a woman from the moment she opened her mouth?

One sees what one wants to see.

One of Landry's mother's favorite sayings trailed through his mind.

Indeed, Mama. Indeed.

He pondered upon his intruder's name for a blink.

Celestia?

An uncommon name for an unusual woman.

At one time or other, while performing scrivener services, Jonathan Tolman had mentioned in passing that he had a daughter. Sons, too, if Landry remembered correctly. Two—both in service to His Majesty's Navy, were they not?

He lifted his eyebrows higher on his forehead.

Truthfully, he wasn't sure whether to be amused or exasperated at Miss Tolman's deception and impertinence.

"Again, I ask, why are you here, Miss Tolman? I

assume you used misleading measures to enter my home?"

A rather charming burst of color tinted her rounded cheeks and spread to her forehead.

To Landry's surprise, she did not cast her gaze downward, clench her hands, or shuffle her feet in embarrassment or shame. Instead, with the artful elegance of a duchess, she hitched her rather adorably mutinous chin and the delightful nub of a nose an inch higher.

"I did, my lord," she boldly confessed. "I pretended to be the sugar delivery boy."

A bark of laughter escaped Landry, and Sampson's tail thudded in happy agreement.

She had put some effort into her deception. Which meant she wasn't as impetuous as he had first supposed.

"Did you now? Mrs. Cox will be beside herself when she learns she has been duped."

A small fission of admiration for Miss Tolman's honesty and straightforwardness sparked behind Landry's ribs.

She was a courageous little thing. Landry would give her that.

"Have a seat." He motioned to the chair. "Please."

The least he could do was hear her out, although he very much suspected he already knew what she would say.

"No, thank you." She shook her head, and her braid bounced against her chest, having the unfortunate effect of dragging his focus to where the coat hid her breasts.

Interest sparked, startling Landry with its intensity. *What the blazes?*

"I am here to ask, my lord, if you would reconsider your decision to discontinue using my father as your scribe," she said in that lyrical contralto, her words sticking slightly on the "my lord" bit.

He filed that detail away to examine later.

Rather than answer her, Landry asked, "Does your father know you are here?"

5

*I know that I am adopted. Mama told me so when I
was a little girl. Right after Papa died, and we
had to leave Lancaster. Who are my real parents?
Why didn't they want me? Who am I really?
Will I ever know? More on point—do I want to?*

~Laureen Smith to her diary

*Keyworth House
Mayfair, London
Still in the Earl of Keyworth's Study*

Miss Tolman neither bristled at the question nor wilted in self-castigation. Instead, she arched a pert, winged eyebrow. With each passing second, Landry found himself ever more intrigued.

"No. My father is unaware I am here, my lord. I came of my own accord."

Making a noncommittal sound in his throat, Landry leaned back and folded his arms.

"Miss Tolman, your father already made the same request of me, and I regret I was compelled to decline."

Two neat lines interrupted the smooth plane of her

forehead, and her stoic composure wavered. To her credit, she swiftly regained her equanimity.

"Yes, yes, I am aware. But since you..."

Fingering her earlobe, Miss Tolman struggled for the appropriate word. Her face cleared, and she continued.

"Dispensed with his services, my lord, our other clientele have also done so at an alarmingly expedient rate. Nearly everyone, in truth."

In point of fact, that reluctant revelation came as no great surprise.

If Tolman had made the same unpardonable mistake with other clients, then he had brought his downfall upon himself. It was deucedly unfortunate that others had to suffer for his incompetence, however. And that Miss Celestia Tolman had to degrade herself and was reduced to sneaking into her father's former client's house.

Nevertheless, Landry could not be held responsible for Jonathan Tolman's ineptitude, his fall from grace, or the reduction in Tolman Tomes—Scrivener and Stationer's clientele.

That blame lay solely at Jonathan Tolman's inebriated feet.

Suddenly restless under Miss Tolman's unrelenting regard, Landry stood.

From across the desk, she stared up at him.

Her almond-shaped green eyes regarded Landry with a mélange of wariness, hope, and antagonism. She reminded him somewhat of a feisty kitten. A small kitten at that.

Crossing to the rosewood liquor cabinet, he asked, "Would you care for a sherry?"

"I beg your pardon?"

"No need to beg, my dear Miss Tolman," he replied rather wickedly, giving into the devil on his shoulder prodding him. Glancing over his shoulder, Landry was very much gratified to see he'd shocked her.

She gaped at him as if he'd sprouted two horns, a forked tail, and cloven hooves.

Perhaps appalled was more apt than shocked.

Giving her his most rakish grin, he held up the crystal decanter. The stopper clinked at his slight jostling. "Sherry?"

"But…" She searched out the mantel clock before turning an incredulous and somewhat censorious gaze upon him. "But it's… It's only just past nine," Miss Tolman said with such incredulousness that Landry could not help but chuckle.

As if she'd never seen her father imbibing so early in the day. A man did not become a sodding drunk like Tolman by restricting his tippling until the evening hours.

"I am aware of the time." He winked just to see her reaction. "You look like you could use a swallow. Perhaps you would prefer something stronger?"

She looked rather taken aback at that suggestion.

Or was it his wink?

"No," she said bluntly before quickly adding, "No, thank you. I do not partake in spirits."

Unlike her sire.

Probably *because* of her sire.

A prim and proper miss was Miss Tolman.

Except for her boy's clothes, sneaking into a peer's house, and being alone with said peer.

Mayhap not so prim and proper after all.

Landry assessed her from beneath half-closed eyes, very much appreciating what he saw.

Reigning in his wayward musings, he said, "Too bad that. You do not know what you are missing."

Did her eyes narrow the merest bit in a silent challenge?

"If by *missing* you mean being irresponsible and negligent, making a general fool of oneself, and otherwise failing to measure up, then I *do* know what I am missing."

The kitten had claws. Sharp claws.

Interesting.

After Landry had poured himself a finger's worth of brandy, he returned to the desk and rested a hip on the edge. He took a sip, welcoming the familiar heat trailing to his stomach.

In truth, it was not his habit to partake of anything more substantial than tea or coffee this early in the day. But Miss Tolman made him edgy in a manner he could not quite put his finger on.

After her outburst, she remained silent, her green eyes alert and keen. She fidgeted with her hat, and her delicate jaw tightened.

Finally, she blurted, "Are you not going to say anything?"

Sampson wandered over and sat next to Landry's feet. He gazed up at him with the adoration and unconditional love only a dog was capable of.

Landry ran his fingers through the dog's fur before shrugging and taking another deep swallow.

"What more is there to say? Your father delivered my transcribed dictation to a courtesan, and her–er *prose* was presented to me. Such colossal mistakes are inexcusable, as I am sure you are aware, Miss Tolman."

Only a slight tightening around her extraordinary eyes indicated his mark had hit home.

"It was the delivery boy's error, but as my father should have brought the documents himself, I acknowledge his culpability. I can assure you that I would personally see that your dictation was securely delivered, and no further mistakes of that unfortunate nature would occur ever again." Head at a proud, nay majestic angle, she said, "I guarantee it."

She seemed quite sincere and not a little desperate.

A tendril of guilt snaked through Landry, and it was not easily squelched.

"Miss Tolman? May I be perfectly candid?"

She met his gaze unflinchingly but without antagonism.

"I would prefer that you were, my lord."

He rather liked that about her.

How she treated him as an equal though they were stations apart.

Most women simpered and batted their eyelashes and either played the coy innocent or issued seductive invitations with their sultry gazes. Miss Celestia Tolman simply looked expectant and, by damn, genuinely unaffected by him or his title.

A rare, *rare* woman indeed.

"When last your father was here, he was well into his cups, Miss Tolman. And I do mean *well* into his cups. Ape drunk is more apt. He even took several generous swallows from his flask during our meeting."

There were two things Landry could not abide: liars

and cheaters. Mr. Jonathan Tolman fell into the former category. He had tried to conceal his failure to deliver Landry's transcriptions and had lied about it. His daughter did not need to know that as well.

Landry had no wish to completely destroy her father's character in her eyes.

"*Oh.*" The single syllable slipped past her lips, part sigh and part exclamation.

Her remarkable eyes—now the color of a forest at sunset—rounded as did her plum red cupid's bow mouth. As if she could not bear his perusal or the stark truth, her lids fluttered closed, her lush eyelashes fanning her cheeks in shadow.

A handful of heartbeats later, Miss Tolman popped her eyes open, her earlier desolation replaced by laudable resolve. As the full comprehension of what Landry had revealed slammed into her, her expression hardened into brittle lines.

Landry would vow, Mr. Jonathan Tolman was due for a severe scold when next she saw her father.

Biting the corner of her lower lip, she averted her gaze for the first time. But only for the span of a heartbeat. Straightening her spine and pushing back her shoulders, she notched that delightfully rebellious chin even higher.

Perhaps to make up for her diminutive height?

If she reached his shoulder, Landry would forgo cake for a week, and he truly revered his sweets.

"I can do the transcribing then," she said. "I have been doing so for eight years. Since I was fifteen."

Well, now Landry knew how old the spitfire was.

Miss Tolman plowed onward in a rush, as if afraid to give him a moment to speak.

"I have been transcribing *all* of my father's work for two years, except for his most prominent clients. Men such as yourself. I have also transcribed numerous documents for my uncle. Contracts, letters, wills, research papers, journals, and much more," she ended a tad breathlessly.

Heartrendingly hopeful. Utterly desperate.

Guilt and compassion coiled even tighter in Landry's gut.

"Very commendable," he murmured at last.

And it was. Astonishing, if he were perfectly candid.

Landry would never know what wicked devil prompted him, but he asked, "And Madame Meriette Bonacieux? Did you transcribe her memoir?"

The transcription had been excellent. Faultless, in truth, as far as Landry could tell. Regardless, what manner of man would permit his daughter to transcribe what could only be described as rather creative sexual exploits?

Miss Tolman bristled, her full mouth firming into two thin lines for an instant as another wave of bright color skated up her pale cheeks. Her freckles stood out in stark relief, a constellation of cinnamon specks on ivory.

Did those delectable freckles cover the rest of her as well?

Are you mad, Keyworth?

"I did," she replied succinctly.

I'll be jiggered.

No virginal lowering of her regard. No dramatics or theatrics that Landry asked such an inappropriate question. A forthright answer.

The truth of it was, Landry needed a scrivener.

Urgently.

But a woman?

Not that he had anything against a woman making her way in the harsh world. Bully for her for having learned the skill. The logistics were what made him hesitant.

Hesitant?

Reluctant. Unwilling. Disinclined.

The phrasing mattered little.

Simply put, what Miss Tolman asked was impossible.

A young, unmarried woman visiting the home of a lord of the realm regularly? At least three times a week for several hours?

No, no. It would not do.

She'd be ruined.

It would not take a week before the *on dit* would label her his mistress.

Landry finished his brandy and set the glass atop the desk.

Mouth pressed into a grim line, he gave a rueful shake of his head.

"I do not think, Miss Tolman, that would be a prudent arrangement for either of us."

He offered a conciliatory smile, hoping to appease her with his charm.

She stood straight and proud, no shoulders slumping in defeat—no pouting or tears. Few noble ladies could boast the regal bearing and demeanor Miss Tolman naturally possessed.

"You are an intelligent woman, Miss Tolman." Landry folded his arms and continued with a slight jutting of his chin in her direction. "I suspect you knew what the outcome must be to both of your requests before you finagled your way into my house."

"I see," she said tautly. Flatly.

He'd bet his best boots every muscle in her small frame was rigid from the control she'd marshaled and the effort to display comportment. Her attention darted to Sampson for a moment, then gravitated back to Landry.

"Might I ask that you at least please stop disparaging Tolman Tomes—Scrivener and Stationer then? As I am sure you are very well aware, it only takes one withering or critical word from a man of your station to your contemporaries to blacken a business's name."

It was Landry's turn to go stiff with affront from head to toe, and he clamped his jaw to bite back his immediate harsh response to her unsavory accusation. Several *tick-tocks* of the longcase clock situated between two of the windows broke the stilted silence before he scratched his nose and relaxed his clenched teeth.

"I give you my word, Miss Tolman. If there is unflattering tattle about your establishment, it did *not* find its beginning with me."

"How can you say that?" she cried, at last losing her composure. "You are the only powerful client who has reason to be dissatisfied with our services."

Arms folded once more, he regarded her.

Her eyes spewed green sparks, and her breasts rose and fell rapidly beneath that godawful coat.

"Are you absolutely positive in that regard, Miss Tolman?"

"Of course, I am..." Her words trailed off, her attention shifting over his shoulder to the gardens. She touched her earlobe again, a crease forming between her eyebrows. "There are children—boys—in your garden."

Landry looked over his shoulder.

Sure enough, a trio of urchins equipped with gardening tools attacked the hedge with the vehemence of inebriated goats. Make that blind, inebriated goats. He cringed inwardly, pitying the poor hedgerow.

"Yes," he said, turning to face her again. "There are."

Miss Tolman cleared her throat before primly saying, "I beg your pardon for interrupting you as well as for entering your home under false pretenses. It may not be any consolation to you, but I am not in the habit of being deceptive."

Her apology was drenched in insincerity.

She was not the least bit regretful, he'd be bound. She believed Landry to be an unfeeling ogre and, at the moment, he rather felt like a troll.

She wound her long braid into a knot with practiced movements before cramming the ugly hat upon her head. Next came the scarf, impossibly uglier than the cap.

"I regret I could not be of service, Miss Tolman."

Landry honestly did have regrets.

What she asked was simply not done.

Hadn't he already come under unfavorable scrutiny for employing as many urchins as he did? Miss Celestia Tolman might be a commoner, but he would not have her reputation besmirched on his account.

She stared at him, the moment stretching on and on, their gazes locked.

Hers accusing and reproachful.

His compassionate and understanding. At least, he hoped that was what Celestia saw because it was what he was feeling and tried to emanate.

It felt as if she peered into his very soul, his spirit. Something—he had no idea what— unlatched. It was the oddest, most penetrating sensation.

Physical, and yet...*not.*

At that moment, Landry knew beyond any vestige of doubt, as improbable and implausible as it was, his life would never be the same. It had shifted course in an unanticipated direction, and he was as helpless as a newborn, sightless kitten to regain control.

And she, Miss Celestia Tolman, with her arresting green eyes, was the reason.

"You *could* have been of service, my lord. You have chosen not to be. I understand and can sincerely appreciate your displeasure. I mistakenly hoped you would be lenient, though I should've known otherwise, given my experience with the nobility."

Landry did not take offense at her well-aimed barb. His refusal to hire Celestia was for her own good. When she had a chance to reflect upon the matter, unless she was a lackwit—which she most assuredly was not—honesty would compel her to accede to the truth.

"I sincerely wish I could have been of assistance," he said, softening his refusal with a smile.

"Please, do not repine on it, my lord."

Her tart riposte was as disingenuous as her earlier apology.

Why Landry should care, he could not begin to fathom.

He forbade himself to.

Miss Celestia Tolman was a stranger. A woman he'd just only met: a woman who had used dishonest measures to enter his home, no less.

And yet…something about her called to him and caused a startling check in his spirit.

He stood and laid his fingertips upon her forearm. Up close, he could see the deeper green that ringed her irises and the citrine flecks shining there.

As if his touch singed or he'd slapped her, she flinched and retreated a pair of steps.

Clearly, she had not experienced the same phenomenon—an awakening in her spirit—an answering vibration in her soul.

That knowledge puzzled and disconcerted him.

"What will you do?" he asked with genuine interest and concern.

"*Do,* my lord?" She raised her impertinent turned-up nose in a lofty manner.

By God, Lady Jersey herself could not have given him a better set down.

"Do you fear I have a vengeful streak, your lordship?"

"Do you?"

"Heaven has no rage like love to hatred turned, nor hell a fury like a woman scorned."

The quote by William Congreve he'd thought of while his mother lay dying intruded upon his contemplation of Miss Tolman.

Landry skewed an eyebrow, several unpleasant scenarios playing out in his mind about how she might retaliate.

Rather than answer, she shrugged. "I have absolutely no idea what I'll do, but I am sure I'll think of something. I'm quite resourceful."

She sliced him a cutting glance meant to eviscerate.

An odd twinge stabbed the region near his heart. In truth, he felt rather badly for Miss Tolman and her situation.

"Perhaps I'll accept Ignatius Cronk's or one of the other gentlemen's offers of a protector," she said with a flippant airiness that did not reach her eyes.

Ballocks to that.

Surely her circumstances were not *that* calamitous?

"Miss Tolman...?"

Landry was about to ask that very thing, but she surprised the starch out of him by dipping into a perfectly orchestrated curtsy. The incongruity of it, such a graceful, ladylike gesture from a hoyden dressed in boy's attire, made him grin despite himself.

"Good day. I'll see myself out," she said crisply, angling toward the French windows. "I pray you lay awake at night pondering if I shall exact revenge upon you."

Was she jesting?

He honestly could not tell.

Instead of exiting through the doorway, she departed through the gardens, taking the time to speak to the eager young chaps as she did.

Chin between his forefinger and thumb, Landry watched her go.

"I think I may have just made the biggest mistake of my life, Sampson."

6

I honestly could use your advice and direction, dear brother. On the infrequent days that Papa does come to the shop, he spends most of his time in his office or the storage area, either drinking himself to oblivion or passed out. Even Uncle Paul is fed up, though with his failing health, his hands are as tied as mine are.

~Letter to Orion Tolman in the service of His Majesty's Navy from his sister Miss Celestia Tolman. Sent but never received

Tolman Tomes—Scrivener and Stationer
Oxford Street, St. Giles, London
13 April 1818

Celestia wrapped the three books, a brass dove-shaped inkwell, feather quills, nibs, and foolscap the Duchess of Westfall had purchased in plain brown paper.

Wearing an exquisite lavender and black walking ensemble, the noblewoman was the embodiment of aristocratic elegance, as were her three companions.

She also smelled positively heavenly.

Celestia had never owned real perfume. The closest she'd ever come was a bottle of lavender rosewater Nash had given her for Christmas the year before Mama died. She found herself inhaling the four duchesses' fragrances, the scents so pleasing that a tiny sliver of envy speared her.

Seldom—almost never, in truth—did Celestia covet *le beau monde* fashions or the female members of the *ton*. She knew her place in society and accepted her circumstance without antipathy. No one had any choice about their birth, whether high born or low.

However, the elegant quartet presently standing before her well-polished but undeniably well-used, scuffed counter made her yearn for something as colorful and stylish as these ladies wore. Her plain ash-gray gown boasted not a single embellishment, and she felt a positive frump compared to their colorful frocks and resplendent bonnets.

English Lavender, sky blue, butterfly yellow, and cranberry red.

A vibrant, fashionable flower garden.

What was more, these ladies were actually pleasant.

Very pleasant and gracious, in truth.

Clustered near the stunningly beautiful Duchess of

Westfall, the equally exquisite Duchesses of Sutcliffe, Bainbridge, and Pennington waited, each with arms full of their purchases. And each looking as if she had stepped directly from an Ackermann's fashion plate.

Never had such prestigious ladies of the *haut ton* frequented Celestia's humble shop.

This made the fourth group of noblewomen this week, and a quartet of duchesses was unprecedented. She was positive not one of them had any need for ink, books, paper, quills, tobacco products, or any other item for sale at Tolman Tomes—Scrivener and Stationer.

Nevertheless, Celestia was not one to look the proverbial gift horse in the mouth.

She did not care *why* the women were here, though she had a pretty good inkling. She'd wager her best gown—a rag compared to the dazzling array before her—the Earl of Keyworth had put his friends' wives up to patronizing the shop.

Interestingly, none of their husbands had stopped in—just the usual male patrons.

Thankfully, not Mr. Cronk or Lord Crocodile as Celestia thought of him because of his propensity to smile broadly, even at inappropriate times.

Humiliation and gratitude wrestled for supremacy

behind her breastbone, and she squeezed her earlobe between her bent forefinger and thumb, slowly massaging the flesh in small circles. She did not know precisely when she'd acquired the habit, but many years ago, she had discovered it calmed her.

Unsurprisingly, gratitude triumphed. Celestia's pride was meaningless if the store closed, which was a genuine possibility at this juncture. Every item sold contributed to the funds for next month's mortgage payment.

What happens after that?

Even the thought made her cringe inwardly. The building was almost paid for. Just another nine months. She must hold on.

Then what?

She honestly and truly did not know.

Giving the Duchess of Bainbridge a bright smile as the lady laid her purchases on the counter, Celestia booted that worry to a dingy corner and covered it with a thick blanket. Tonight, as she lay in bed awake once more, troublesome thoughts parading through her mind, she'd have plenty of time to examine that concern.

The bell attached to the door gave a happy little jingle as yet another customer entered. Today was the busiest day Tolman Tomes—Scrivener and Stationer had experienced in weeks.

From Celestia's position behind the counter, she could not see who the patron was. For some time now, she'd wanted to rearrange the shop's interior since anymore, more often than not, she was alone. Well, at least alone on the ground floor.

This arrangement had worked well when Mama and Aunt Rosalie both worked here as their husbands transcribed in the offices above. However, now that Celestia operated the establishment by herself most days, she really required a vantage point where she could observe the entire sales floor.

In recent weeks Celestia had considered changing the establishment's name to Tolman Tomes and Tobacco since, at present, no transcribing took place. It wasn't probable that it would in the future either, and she still partially blamed Keyworth for that.

However, his question about whether she was certain Papa had not made other mistakes niggled like an annoying pebble in her shoe. The truth of it was, she could not be absolutely positive he had not.

Would Papa destroy correspondences terminating his services so she would not know? The man he had been before Mama's death would never have.

But now…?

After her unpleasant and unproductive visit to the Earl of Keyworth's home, Celestia had confronted her father. He admitted to having arrived half-foxed to request his position back.

"Just needed a little nip to bolster my courage, my girl," he claimed, looking sheepish.

Exhausted and downtrodden because of her constant worry, Celestia had finally lost her temper.

"We are on the verge of ruin, Papa! I can barely make the mortgage payment each month."

"Surely not," he muttered, his ruddy face etched in disbelief.

"I am not exaggerating. You must put aside your spirits and focus on your work once more. If not for yourself or me, then for Mama. She would've been heartily ashamed of you. Your grief isn't an excuse to remain foxed and avoid your responsibilities."

Born out of frustration and panic, that last accusation had been unfair and unkind. A yoke of shame and regret weighed heavily upon Celestia. She was abashed that she'd spoken to him so harshly, though she still believed he'd needed to confront the truth.

Regardless, her dust-up had served no useful purpose. Her father had simply hung his head and shoulders slumped, made for the nearest pub. Or wherever it was that he procured his gin.

As far as changing the shop's name went, Papa and Uncle would have to agree. Plus, that would require funds she could not spare to have a new sign made and the window painted. So, like so many other things she'd wished for, considered, or wanted, she filed the idea away.

Perhaps someday.

She cast a swift glance to the narrow stairway leading to the upper rooms. Papa's and Uncle's offices were overhead, as well as a large storage area with a cot. Three other rooms sat empty.

The previous proprietor had lived above the shop with his wife, but when Papa and Uncle Paul bought the building nearly five-and-twenty years ago, Mama had declared the space too small for a family and insisted they live in a real house.

Jonathan Tolman had stumbled in three hours ago and had staggered directly upstairs, as was his wont these past weeks. As usual, he had not offered to help.

However, as soused as he was, he would not have

been of any assistance in any event.

How much longer could this go on?

She'd taken to hiding the earnings each day to keep him from pilfering the funds away on spirits. Where he had obtained the coins for his current bout of drunkenness, she couldn't fathom.

Uncle Paul had stayed home today as well. His gout had been a terrible trial of late. When he had an onset, nothing but bed rest and elevating his affected foot would do. Cold compresses brought him a small degree of relief too.

Childless, he regarded her as the daughter he never had. Between fretting over Papa's drinking, Uncle Paul's health, the fate of the store, and her unanswered letters to her brothers, Celestia was a jumble of nerves.

"I am so delighted I came today," Her Grace, the Duchess of Pennington, said while examining her purchases.

Shrugging off her doldrums, Celestia smiled.

"As am I, Your Grace," she said, wrapping a silver cigar nipper. "I am extremely honored."

"Keyworth," exclaimed the Duchess of Bainbridge. "I'm so happy you stopped by."

He was here?

Oh, Lord. No. Just what I need.

"Thank you for recommending this delightful establishment," her grace said. "I have been trying to find this exact shade of sealing wax for ages."

"Did not I tell you this establishment's inventory was exceptional?" came Landry's melodic baritone.

"Indeed, you did," agreed one of the duchesses.

Celestia had no idea which lady because she refused to raise her attention from the brown paper she expertly wrapped the snuff box in.

"Miss Tolman is also an accomplished scrivener, should you require the services of an amanuensis," he said a trifle too casually and with a distinct droll edge to his tenor.

"How fascinating," replied another duchess, sounding anything but.

Dratted man.

Most of the time, ladies of quality wrote their own correspondence and those that did not hired a secretary.

Was Lord Keyworth determined to humiliate her?

Keyworth, I have done a bit of poking around on your behalf, and I believe I have found just the fellow for you. His name is Marshall Britmere. He has gained a reputation as a brilliant investigator— a master sleuth, if you will.

~Letter to the Earl of Keyworth from the Duke of Westfall

Tolman Tomes—Scrivener and Stationer
(Soon to be Tolman Tomes and Tobacco?)
Oxford Street, St. Giles
A Few Extremely Awkward Minutes Later

Celestia's heart flopped around behind her ribs like a dying trout before diving straight to her stomach as if weighted by a lodestone.

Why was the earl here?

She was equal parts appreciative and vexed. Excited and trepidatious.

That annoying man had her at sixes and sevens.

Landry, Earl of Keyworth, had snarled her in more complicated knots than those her seafaring brothers had shown her. Keeping her focus pointed at the new group of items that required wrapping, she steadfastly refused to meet his penetrating, pewter gaze.

Yet, despite deliberately ignoring him, she felt his potent visual touch as forcefully as when he'd touched her arm in his office.

Her stupid, gullible heart had thrashed about her chest like a terrified fox in a basket that day. How could the merest wisp of his fingertips threaten to incinerate her? She'd nearly gone up in a sizzling conflagration of sensation.

No doubt existed that he observed her with that disarming twinkle in his eye and his mouth tilted in that rakish manner.

I shall not look.

I. Shall. Not.

The duchesses chatted about their children, where they intended to have a spot of tea this afternoon, and the Duke of Asherford's dinner party next week.

"You are attending, are you not, Keyworth?" the Duchess of Westfall inquired as she secured her reticule's silk ribbons. "Ansley and Willow are as well."

"Indeed, I am," the earl replied. "I quite look forward to seeing your brother. I have a matter I wished to discuss with Scarborough."

The Duchess of Sutcliffe laughed and shook her

head. "I'll venture it has something to do with that project you've been working on for Parliament."

He chuckled, that delicious rumble reverberating in his chest. "Perhaps."

"I vow I shall tell my husband to prohibit any talk of politics," the Duchess of Westfall teased.

Celestia managed to avoid looking in Landry's direction until she'd tied the last string on the Duchess of Sutcliffe's purchases.

He leaned casually against the counter, his hat tilted at a rakish angle, and that playful, arrogant, devastating smile notching his mouth up at one corner.

Must he be so deucedly attractive?

Just when she convinced herself he was a complete ogre, entirely irredeemable, he'd done something kind and generous.

You knew the moment you discovered he regularly helped street urchins that his heart is not entirely black.

True. And the earl needn't have recommended the shop to his illustrious contemporaries, and yet he had.

Why?

Guilt?

No, he had no cause to feel guilty.

Everything he'd said to her last week had been correct.

After Celestia had reflected upon it, she'd been

forced to acknowledge that truth. Papa's unprofessional behavior had brought them to this juncture. The earl had no choice but to dismiss him.

Keyworth's reputation was at stake too.

That did not make it any easier to accept, however.

"Thank you, Your Graces," she said as they gathered their purchases and edged toward the entrance.

"Rest assured, Miss Tolman, I, for one, intend to return often." Her face swathed in a warm smile, the Duchess of Bainbridge canted her head.

"As do I," echoed the other ladies.

They took their leave, and Celestia busied herself tidying up the counter. After she'd rolled the string up and put away the scissors, she faced the earl.

"Did you need something, my lord? Or did you just stop by to see if your benevolent efforts were successful?"

He grinned, not at all put off by her starchy tone.

"Have they been?"

He brushed a piece of lint from his charcoal gray coat, accented by black velvet cuffs and lapels. Understated elegance and powerful masculine grace. She'd never considered a man graceful before, but after seeing him in his office, she could think of no other appropriate description.

He moved with lithe, lean, smooth measures, and

an undercurrent of powerful male fairly oozed from him. Never had a man so rattled her. As much as she loathed admitting it, she, a prim and proper bluestocking, was hard-pressed not to stare like a gawping schoolgirl.

His features were not precisely handsome in the conventional sense. They were far too rugged for that. Yet the straight blade of his nose, the strong, angular jaw with the faintest hint of whiskers, a well-formed mouth that had the vexing tendency to twitch with amusement, and his hawkish dark sable eyebrows melded together to create a fine specimen of manhood.

Very fine, indeed.

His finest features, though, were his endless eyes.

In short, they were beautiful. Stunningly so.

Gray ringed with midnight blue and shards of silvery-blue fringed by thick, sooty lashes—she felt as if she were sinking each time she gazed into them. At first, she'd believed his eyes were pale blue. In some light, they appeared silver.

No, quicksilver.

His intense gaze probed hers. Asking, taking, and something else glinted in those depths that Celestia could not, for the life of her, identify.

Lifting a shoulder, she brushed away paper residue from the shiny wood. "I appreciate any business, so I thank you. However, you should be aware, ladies of the *ton*, in general, have no need of an amanuensis."

"Not even for their memoirs?" Landry asked, giving her a rakish, lopsided smile.

The devil.

Fire burned in Celestia's cheeks, for she knew full well what he referred to, the scoundrel.

"A gentleman would not remark upon *that*," she said, frost edging her words.

"I think it admirable," he said in apparent seriousness. "And you've done nothing to color about."

Now he was lying through his perfectly even and annoyingly white teeth.

They both knew how utterly inappropriate it was for Celestia to have transcribed Madame Bonacieux's memoir. The experience had been…educational and enlightening.

Celestia gravitated her focus to the storefront, where a young couple stood arm in arm outside, perusing the window display. The man said something, and the woman turned her adoring gaze up to his.

Celestia felt like an interloper and resolutely turned her thoughts to today's sales.

Despite Landry's steering business in the shop's direction, she knew—in the deepest recesses of her soul—it would not be enough.

Sudden weariness engulfed her, and a flood of hot tears sprang to her eyes. She swiftly lowered her lashes, lest he see.

Drat. Drat. Drat.

Celestia did not weep in public. Ever.

She was a strong, self-sufficient woman, and by Jiminy, she would not cry.

It must be a lack of sleep. She lay awake each night, staring at the cracked ceiling and worrying about her future and Papa's and Uncle Paul's too.

Neither Orion nor Nash had answered her last three letters.

What could they do anyway?

Nothing, devil it. Not a dashed thing.

Neither of her brothers had any desire to take on the store's operation, and both loved the navy, so she suspected they'd make it their careers.

Perhaps she could talk Papa and Uncle Paul into selling the house. The shop's upper story could be transformed into living accommodations again. It mightn't be as comfortable as their current home, but it was better than losing their income source.

For the second time in less than half an hour, she grasped her earlobe and gently rotated the flesh between her fingers.

"You do that when you are tense or agitated,"

Keyworth said matter of factly.

What?

"Do what?"

He gave a pointed look at her fingers massaging her earlobe. At once, she dropped her hand to her side.

Never before had anyone noticed or commented on her habit.

Not her mother or father.

Not her older brothers, who loved nothing better than to tease her.

No one until this irksome man had taken note. And not only took note but rudely remarked upon it.

Well, you, my lord, quirk your eyebrows and mouth in a most arrogant fashion ALL of the time.

Leveling him a bland look, she said, "My lord, I have tasks that need my attention."

Dusting the shelves was not a pressing chore, but the earl affected her most curiously, and she needed the distraction.

"I have a proposition for you, Miss Tolman."

8

*I should never have visited the Earl of Keyworth.
I want to hate him as I did before, but I now know
he's not the blackguard I once believed him to be.
I cannot stop thinking about him.*

Miss Celestia Tolman to her diary

*Tolman Tomes—Scrivener and Stationer
Oxford Street, St. Giles
Several More Impossibly Uncomfortable Minutes Later*

Celestia went utterly still, despair sluicing through her, shredding the last remnants of hope that the Earl of Keyworth wasn't an opportunistic libertine.

Lord, not him too?

Was that why he'd refused to hire Papa back or retain her services.

She felt all of the color drain from her face as she permitted her eyelids to drift shut and block his handsome visage.

Why should he be any different? her cryptic conscience scolded.

Kicking her disappointment aside, she dredged up

her fractured composure and opened her eyes.

"I am not interested," she stated flatly. Icily. Loading those four words with as much disdain and scorn as she could muster.

"You do not even know what I was going to suggest," Keyworth said, his eyebrow cocked in that skeptical, faintly mocking manner she'd already come to know.

Plunking her hands on her hips, Celestia glowered, far past the point of politesse, lord or no lord.

"Don't I?" She jabbed an ink-stained finger at his chest, taking a measure of satisfaction when he retreated a step. Never mind that her finger throbbed where she'd encountered an inflexible wall of solid muscle.

He blinked at her in bewilderment, as if she'd impaled him with a sword.

Oh, he was good.

So very good.

Acting the innocent. The imposed upon victim.

"You'll offer me a tidy sum," she snapped. "A few jewels or bric-a-brac. Perhaps a carriage and team for my use, along with a *charming* little house in an older but *respectable* part of town."

Utter shock flitted across his chiseled features, and the earl's jaw slackened comically. If she weren't so riled, she might actually have been amused.

"You think…?" Lord Keyworth stuttered, shaking his head and waving his hands before him. "By God, I am not…"

Just short of rolling his eyes, he pointed his gaze toward the ceiling for a blink.

"*Blessed Jesus*," he practically growled.

Was that a prayer or an expletive?

Lord Keyworth inhaled a steadying breath and shook his dark head again.

"Miss Tolman, I give you my word as a gentleman. I am *not* asking you to become my mistress."

His cheeks were suspiciously rosy. As if *he* were genuinely embarrassed.

Impossible.

Rakes and rogues and flirtatious rapscallions such as he did not blush.

Eyes narrowed to furious slits and hands balled into fists, she glared daggers at him.

"You are *not*?"

"Indeed, no. I would never be so degrading." His quicksilver gaze searched hers, and the intensity there made her want to squirm. "Have you had…that is, I presume you have been made such insulting offers before?"

She gave a stiff nod. "I have. Several times, in fact."

The air chuffed from his lungs. His expression turned to stone, and flinty fury glinted in his eyes.

"Who?"

One short, steely syllable. Landry seemed genuinely offended on her behalf.

"Why should you care?"

"I care that any woman is imposed upon in such a debasing and demeaning manner."

She laughed then, disbelieving and shrill.

"Are you telling me you've *never* kept a mistress, my lord? I thought all lords ran through lovers as swiftly as bluestockings read books."

His mouth quipped upward, and the seductive twinkle returned to his gray eyes. "That, Miss Tolman, is an interesting analogy."

She felt the unflattering flush mounting from her chest to her hairline. *Again.*

Her face probably looked like a radish by now.

Celestia did not blush daintily like the lovely English roses who'd just left her shop. She turned raspberry red from her bosoms to her hairline. It was most aggravating and gave her every emotion away.

"You avoided the question, my lord."

"As any gentleman should," he remarked unapologetically while regarding her in such a penetrating fashion, she felt… Well, she did not have a name for whatever this warm, unnerving feeling was.

Smoothing her skirt, she deliberately changed the subject. "Your…ah…proposition?"

"I should like you to transcribe my speeches and letters for me," he announced succinctly. "As you say, the duchesses have little need for a scrivener, and I have a pressing need for one."

Celestia's jaw went slack, and her heart somersaulted with excitement. And hope.

Precious, improbable hope.

Was it possible?

Had he *really* reconsidered?"

"But…but you said I could not come to your residence," she said, gripping the countertop so hard her knuckles turned white.

Which, as she reflected upon it later, would never have worked.

Who would've run the store in her absence?

She'd have to close it during those times she transcribed, and they could not afford that.

"And you shan't." He looked around the small

space. "I presume this establishment has an office?"

Nodding, she said, "Two, actually. Upstairs."

She directed her gaze to the narrow stairway at the back of the room behind the counter.

"Well, then. We shall use one for our purposes. Your father or uncle can act as a chaperone." Forehead knitted, he perused the shop. "You are alone?"

"My father is upstairs. He's…"

She lifted a helpless gaze to him, the shame settling on her like a heavy, familiar cloak.

Pity darkened Landry's gray eyes to charcoal. She hated that he so readily understood the futility of her situation. Pity stripped a person of their dignity, no matter that it came couched as compassion and kindness.

"I spoke with Papa after I visited with you." Lips pursed, Celestia shook her head. "As much as I wish otherwise, our conversation was not productive."

"And your uncle?" he asked, seemingly sincerely interested.

"He's been unwell too, I fear."

"Hmm." Landry made that inarticulate sound in the back of his throat that he made when he was thinking.

"I know two trustworthy, hardworking lads, each

sixteen or seventeen years old, that could act as sales clerks when you are transcribing for me," he put forth.

"No." Mortification scalding her cheeks, Celestia shook her head and wet her lower lip. "The shop is not in a financial position to pay anyone wages."

"You would not have to," Landry replied easily. "I have placed several older boys and girls in respectable establishments to learn various trades, rather like apprenticeships. I pay their wages during training, and quite often, their employers are so pleased they offer them full-time positions."

Why, Celestia had never heard of such a thing.

Utterly flummoxed and momentarily rendered speechless, she, at last, found her tongue. "That is very generous of you and, I must admit, quite unusual as well as philanthropic."

"So, are you interested?" Landry pressed, a glint of expectation in his kind eyes.

Celestia searched his face for any indication of deception or mockery. Any hint of jesting or taunting.

There wasn't any.

Just sincere, heartfelt regard that made her feel at once very feminine and extremely maladroit.

How could she ever have believed him hard-hearted or uncaring?

She had observed him being the epitome of kindness, benevolence, and consideration in all things. Such characteristics were unusual, most especially in a privileged lord of the realm.

Celestia's admiration and respect grew markedly stronger.

"I'll pay you the same fees I paid your father," he said.

Hope flared behind Celestia's ribs again, and a wave of relief unfurled in her belly.

It might, *just might*, be enough to keep the shop running until the mortgage was paid in full. Nine months was not so very long.

She fashioned her mouth into the first authentic smile of the afternoon and extended her hand.

"I accept, my lord."

Landry glanced at her gloveless, outstretched hand and then, flashing her a blinding, incandescent grin, clasped her hand firmly in his big palm.

A jolt shot up her arm to her shoulder and then spread, a scintillating electrical current throughout her body.

Well, one thing was for certain, she conceded once

her pulse had returned to a semblance of normal. She would *never* be bored with Landry, Earl of Keyworth, about. No, bored was the farthest thing from what she was feeling at the moment.

"I think we shall get along very well, Celestia," he said in that warm-honeyed baritone that caused all sorts of peculiar reactions from the hair rising along her nape in awareness to a most discomfiting sensation low in her abdomen.

Perhaps, far too well.

And yet, that sardonic thought did not disturb or unnerve Celestia nearly as much as it ought to have done. Would have done a mere week ago.

"I shall call tomorrow at three if that time is convenient for you." Mouth tilted into a lopsided smile, Landry glanced toward the door and then back at her. "I'll bring the lads with me."

9

Your Lordship, I have most excellent news!
I have been able to locate a former parishioner
of Reverend Smythe-Shufflebottom in Lancaster.
The elderly woman corresponds with a Ruth Smith,
though irregularly. Mrs. Smith and her daughter,
Laureen, currently live in Brighton. I believe
Mrs. Smith is, in fact, Mrs. Smythe-Shufflebottom,
and her daughter is your sister, Lenora.

~Letter to the Earl of Keyworth from Marshall
Britmere, investigator

Still at Tolman Tomes—Scriveners and Stationer
Oxford Street, St. Giles, London
And Still 13 April 1818

Landry skewed his mouth into a lopsided smile as Celestia licked her lower lip, then gave a hesitant nod. "That should suffice. I'll inform my father and uncle."

Attempting to ignore the immediate and powerful surge of lust to his groin when her tongue darted out, he focused his attention on what she'd said.

Why had her uncle and father let her bear the brunt of the store's operations?

It was not that Landry did not think Celestia capable. She'd proven she was a most resourceful and intrepid female. No, what rankled him was slugabed men who thought nothing of letting a woman shoulder most of the burden.

Such men deserved no respect.

Neither did the cads who had propositioned her. He would have their names from her eventually, and when he did…

Well, they would not trouble her with their uncouth suggestions ever again.

He would also wager his beloved Sampson that Celestia did the brunt of the shopping, cooking, and housework too. Beneath her magnificent, intelligent eyes, faint purplish half-moon shadows contrasted with her ivory skin.

In truth, she looked done in. And indescribably beautiful.

The urge to shield her from harm burgeoned inside him, a wildfire building in intensity and power until it consumed Landry. No woman other than his mother and, to a degree, the sister he'd never met had ever stirred such protective sentiments.

That was one of the reasons he'd imposed upon the

wives of several friends to frequent Tolman Tomes—Scrivener and Stationer. Other than a few elevated eyebrows, quirked mouths, and speaking glances amongst his chums, they had prudently kept their thoughts to themselves and readily complied with his request.

That was what good friends did.

Supported one another without question.

Although Landry knew full well they were dying to learn the whole of it. And no doubt, after today, he'd face an inquisition the next time he encountered those duchesses. At some future juncture, he would have to explain everything.

God save his soul.

Tucking a stray strand of treacle brown hair behind her ear, Celestia filled her lungs with a deep breath. His gaze slipped to the voluptuous bounty hidden beneath the plain fabric of her gown.

Damn my eyes.

Despite his determination to be a gentleman and not ogle her like a delicacy displayed at a pastry shop, his focus repeatedly dipped to her ample bosom. Celestia might be small in stature, but Landry would vow she possessed a very womanly form. Even her gown, a drab gray affair, could not detract from her luscious curves or her unpretentious beauty.

"I wonder if you'd do me the courtesy of answering a personal question, Miss Tolman?"

She had begun dusting the countertop and paused, glancing up at him, her gaze unwavering. A tiny, puzzled frown drew her delicate eyebrows together.

"I suppose that depends on the question. I'd be an addlepate to blindly agree without knowing what it is you want to know."

Unable to fully check his grin, Landry scratched his nose.

Verbal sparring with her was quite refreshing and entertaining.

"Your name. It is quite unusual. I have not heard it before. Is it a family name?"

Her low, melodic laugh caused something to unfurl deep inside him. Its strands wound around him, ensnaring him in warmth and wonder.

"No. My mother was an amateur astrologer. My brothers' names are Nash and Orion—both other names for star. Mama adored studying the constellations and stars." She angled her chin toward a bookshelf. "We still stock a selection of books on astronomy. I believe she read every one of them at least twice."

"Fascinating," Landry said.

Setting aside her dust cloth, Celestia's expression grew pensive. "That is a wonderful advantage of owning a used bookstore. I am never without reading material."

"Your mother sounds like a remarkable woman. How long ago did you lose her?" he asked with sincere interest.

A fragile half-smile bent her rosy mouth upward, and sadness darkened her eyes. "She was the most intelligent woman I have ever known. She passed three years ago from cancer after a long illness. She was only six-and-forty."

Landry made a sympathetic noise in his throat. They had more in common than he would have ever supposed. "I, too, lost my mother from cancer. She was two-and-forty. We were very close as well."

"I am sorry." Compassion softened her mouth and the corners of her eyes. "Have you other family?"

Landry was astounded to realize he wanted Celestia to know about Lenora. He had not even shared his sister's existence with his closest friends until recently. To be precise, until he'd been required to seek their advice about retaining a new investigator.

"None except a half-sister that I have been trying to locate for eight years."

Celestia's eyes grew round with disbelief, and she inhaled a short, sharp gasp.

"You do not *know* where she is?" she asked incredulously.

Shaking his head, he said, "Not for certain. I have had an investigator searching for her ever since I learned of her existence eight years ago."

He brushed a black-gloved fingertip back and forth below his nose before responding.

"Lenora was not my father's child."

No disdain or shock marred Celestia's features. Rather, she laid her hand on his forearm and gave a small, sympathetic squeeze. A jolt not unlike the time lightning had struck a tree a half-mile away out of the blue when he'd been out riding sluiced through him.

Every hair on his body had stood on end then too.

What was it about this woman that had him so mesmerized?

Celestia Tolman was a perplexing, tantalizing enigma that he yearned to unwrap and explore. And yet, he knew he must proceed with caution. She was wary of men. Justifiably, given what she'd disclosed a few minutes ago about the multiple offers of protectors.

A nice word for a pimp, just as a kept mistress was a polite word for prostitute.

Landry wanted to know everything about Celestia, and that was a first for him.

Her station meant less than nothing to him.

What she did to him *did* matter. Rather a lot, actually.

Removing her hand from his arm, Celestia gave a little self-conscious smile, as if she'd suddenly realized she'd overstepped the mark. Clearing her throat, she picked up her dust cloth once more.

"Until tomorrow then, your lordship," she said primly, clearly bringing their discussion, and thereby his visit, to a conclusion.

Removing his hat, Landry bent into a gallant bow. "I eagerly anticipate it."

Very much indeed.

She blinked and then, a mischievous grin arcing her mouth, dipped into a perfect curtsy.

It was his turn to blink in astonishment.

Her entire demeanor transformed, and she had become a teasing vixen.

"None of that. I do not intend to stand on formality

falderol." He winked and was delighted to see two charming spots of color spring to life on her cheeks.

"Good day, Celestia."

Her eyes went wide at the familiarity. However, she did not chastise Landry, though from the way she clamped her bottom lip with her teeth, the thought had occurred to her. For whatever reason, she'd eschewed doing so.

Good, because he intended for them to be on a given name basis.

He exited the store, feeling more satisfied than he had in a good while. And also quite positive he'd just put something in motion he could not control nor stop. What was more, he was not altogether certain he wanted to do either.

Whistling a bawdy tavern ditty, Landry mounted Fie, his black gelding, and turned the horse in the direction of the Wicked Earls' Club.

Ridiculously happy—almost giddy—Landry grinned like a Cheshire cat.

Celestia had agreed to transcribe for him.

His guilt for sending her packing without hope or recourse slid from his shoulders like a discarded cloak.

"I pray you lay awake at night pondering if I shall

exact revenge upon you."

She had exacted her revenge, just not in the manner Landry had expected. And he did lay awake at night, but not for the reasons she had no doubt anticipated.

Miss Celestia Tolman had disrupted his life, his sleep, and his future. But what an incredible, extraordinarily welcome disruption.

Landry's meeting with Sharonford had not been as productive as he'd have liked, but later that afternoon at White's, he'd encountered the Duke of Westfall. It turned out Westfall had been most helpful, and within four-and-twenty hours Marshall Britmere had departed London in search of Lenora.

Britmere had a stellar reputation as an investigator. To date, he hadn't failed at a single assignment. His fee was exorbitant, but he also guaranteed his work— something no other detective offered and which also testified to Britmere's confidence and expertise.

No wonder Madagan had not been able to find Lenora, not that he'd tried overly hard, truth be told. He had become accustomed to slugging along on Landry's coin. Once he located Lenora, he would've put himself out of a cushy job. Therefore, he had only sent along tidbits to keep Landry's appetite whetted but never enough to actually solve the case of his missing sister.

He was out of a position now, nevertheless.

Lenora's adopted mother had changed her name when she was first taken in. Later, after her husband died, Mrs. Smith had dropped the latter part of her surname and changed the first part's spelling. Which, given the nature of and reason for her wayward spouse's demise, was not at all shocking or astonishing.

It seems the cleric's paramour—a buxom tavern maid he had got with child—had pushed him down the parish's back stairs when he refused to leave his wife and adopted daughter.

Landry kicked himself to next Sunday and back for not having hired a different investigator sooner. Lenora might have been safely ensconced beneath his roof and under his care and protection years ago had he done so.

In a single day, his life seemed to be falling into order.

His sister might very well be found, and he had come up with a viable solution to his need for a scrivener and Celestia's need for funds. She'd be in high dudgeon if she knew he had poked around a bit regarding the Tolmans' finances.

Neither of the Tolman elder brothers was a gambler

nor a wastrel, and neither had outstanding debts, aside from the building's mortgage. A mortgage which Landry had paid off but had made the bank swear not to inform the Tolmans—or anyone else for that matter.

Instead, the remaining monthly payments were to be deposited in an account in Celestia's name. Somehow, Landry knew in his gut that she would not appreciate his high-handedness. Regardless, he could not squelch his ever-increasing instinct to protect her.

It is bloody well more than that, and you well know it.

Indeed, he did.

Yesterday, he'd finally admitted the truth to himself.

He, Landry Garrad Jeremy Audsley, Earl of Keyworth, had a romantic interest in Celestia Tolman. Not just an idle, passing fancy that would slake him physically. No, this allure went much farther than mere carnal desire.

A ridiculous, farcical notion had begun rattling around in his head days ago, and the memory of an oath he'd made to himself years before bobbed to the forefront of his mind once more.

By God, I would marry a flower hawker or a

seamstress if she loved me, and I loved her.

Or a petite bluestocking scrivener?

Aye. A prim and proper and utterly enchanting, breathtaking, incomparable bluestocking. All the better that she could act as his amanuensis. Theirs would be a perfect partnership if he did say so himself.

Several people gave him odd looks as if he were bosky as he trotted Fie along the busy lane.

It may have had to do with the ridiculous grin splitting his face from ear to ear.

It had been a very long time since he'd anticipated anything as much as his appointment with Celestia Tolman tomorrow afternoon.

10

Once my service in the navy is over in June, I may stay in the Americas, Tia. There are many opportunities in this country, the likes of which I cannot hope to achieve in England. You know I have never been interested in the store or scribing. Do not say anything to Papa just yet. I know he'll object.

Letter from Orion Tolman to his sister Celestia Tolman
Sent early April 1818 but not received

Tolman Tomes—Scrivener and Stationer
Oxford Street, St. Giles, London
6 May 1818

Bent over her father's serviceable desk, Celestia waited for Landry to proceed with his dictation. The chair's cracked leather protested as she shifted her position to better catch the light from the small window behind her. Once a cheerful yellow, the faded and chipped paint had mellowed into sallow saffron and did little to brighten the chamber's dingy atmosphere.

Today's document was a draft of a petition Landry meant to circulate to support workhouse and child labor reformations. She admired him for his lofty goals, though if she were wholly forthright, she doubted he would muster the backing he required.

In her experience, people adored the pretense of munificence, benevolence, and charity. As long as it did not require any real degree of sacrifice or commitment on their part.

All of the accolades of a saint without any of the discomforts, she thought bitterly.

Neck bent, his thumb and forefinger cradling his chin, Landry paced back and forth. His glossy Hessians rapped rhythmically upon the wood floor, a comforting cadence.

Celestia could not help but admire the tautness of his superfine forest green coat as it stretched across his broad back and shoulders. Nor the biceps straining the fabric of his jacket or the rippling muscles of his thighs encased in black trousers.

He moved with a lithe sinewiness, an ebb and flow of stark masculinity that beckoned to her femininity on a primal level. She was unsure if he was aware of the effect he had on women, or if perhaps she was simply more susceptible to his manliness than other females.

Because, stupid and foolish and preposterous though it was, she'd come to care for him these past weeks. Care for him a great deal, in point of fact.

Inhaling a steadying breath, she ceased her clandestine examination of the much too good-looking and far too distracting earl. Stifling a sigh for which she could not name the cause, she attended to the foolscap before her.

Quill poised, Celestia fingered an earlobe and waited.

"Therefore," Landry said, one forefinger raised and his voice ringing with conviction and authority, "it is the intrinsic responsibility, the ethical duty, and the moral obligation to help those amongst us who cannot help themselves. To whom much is given, much shall be required."

Pride thrummed through her, bringing a nascent smile as she carefully penned the shorthand.

He is a good man.

Landry was indeed a decent man—peer or not— and shame swept her that she'd ever believed otherwise. She had judged him without knowing all of the facts. Condemned him because it was easier to blame someone else than look closer to home to where the real culpability lay.

Wasn't that just like human nature?

To see the flaws in others so clearly while turning

a blind eye to one's own, often far worse, faults?

How drastically things had changed since Celestia had sneaked into Landry's home and his big dog had terrified her. Sampson had visited Tolman Tomes—Scrivener and Stationer several times now.

He was every bit as gentle as Landry had vowed.

Indeed, the very man she would've relegated to hell's bowels without a qualm four weeks ago was now the person she most looked forward to seeing. He, quite literally, had brightened her dreary life to such a degree she could not comprehend returning to her former drudgery.

It did not bear thinking upon.

Landry had become a vital—no, *the* vital—part of her life.

They had fallen into a comfortable routine these past three weeks. He arrived in the afternoon Mondays, Tuesdays, and Wednesdays and dictated for two, three, or occasionally four hours. The rest of the week, she transcribed his work and presented the finished notes to him the next Monday.

If he needed to add a thought or if she required clarification, they sent notes back and forth several more times throughout the week. She looked forward to those brusque but polite missives without a trace of the poetic or a romantic vein with the same anticipation as receiving a lace-edged Valentine.

Not that she'd ever received such a novelty.

Regardless, she had seen them displayed in the picture windows of various establishments year after year near Valentine's Day. Every year, she coveted one for herself from her very own sweetheart.

Never before had the days inched by so exasperatingly slowly as they did between Landry's visits. Celestia found herself fussing over her appearance and had even remade two of her mother's gowns in the evenings after work—one in seafoam green and another in midnight blue.

There also remained a lovely berry red gown trimmed in euchre lace she thought to attempt to make into a more formal affair, but her seamstress skills were not her greatest strength.

Even as she took extra care with her appearance and worked her needle in and out, in and out, in the parlor each evening, she knew full well she had set upon a fool's journey. A sojourn that could only lead to heartache and regret.

Fine then.

Celestia would take whatever she could because all too soon this man who made her heart sing and blood tingle, who had crept into her dreams at night and tangled her thoughts during the day, might be gone from her life.

Forever.

These memories would have to sustain her.

Today, Celestia had dared to wear the green gown and had even threaded a matching ribbon in her new, less severe hairstyle. A few curls brushed her ears and framed her face. Her mother's pearl earrings hung from her ears, and a simple, single strand of pearls graced her neck.

She felt pretty and elegant.

And rather silly, like a dressed-up doll. And not a little vulnerable.

Would Landry see through her playacting?

Understand it for what it was?

An attempt to appear attractive for him?

Of course, Celestia understood she could never compare to the chic ladies of *le beau monde* draped in their first stares of fashion. Nevertheless, for a bluestocking shopkeeper, she supposed—*hoped*—she measured up satisfactorily.

A simple shawl wrapped around her shoulders helped to keep the ever-present drafts at bay. A tiny thrill rushed through her as she recalled that several times this afternoon, she had observed Landry's smoldering gaze wandering to the skin exposed above her bodice.

Not in a leering or lecherous way, as had the other men who had stared at her breasts. Those men made her want to hide or cover herself or take a bath and scrub her skin until it glowed pink.

Landry's male appreciation did not make her feel any of those things.

There was another gleam in his gray eyes. A glint that darkened them to pewter, except for the silver flecks that sparked and glimmered.

That look made her shiver, and not from cold either.

Celestia castigated herself for allowing the Earl of Keyworth to wriggle his way into her heart in such a short time. She, a prim and proper bluestocking, knew better than to permit a handsome man to charm her. To seduce her into casting aside common sense and practicality. To long for that which could never, ever be.

There was nothing the least bit prim and proper about the dreams she'd had the past few nights, however. Dreams that awakened her after midnight and left her…wanting…wanting…

Good God and sweet Jesus too.

Heat suffused her, and she ducked her head for fear her fiery cheeks would give her away. A draft would be most welcome at this moment. Alas, at this precise interlude, the upper room remained draft-free for the first time in weeks.

Curling her toes into her shoes until they cramped, Celestia tightened her fingers on the quill, pressing the nib so hard it snapped.

Blast.

She did not know *what* it was exactly that she wanted when she awoke sweaty and tense and aching. Nevertheless, she was confident the peculiar throbbing sensation had something to do with Landry.

And the way he surreptitiously watched her.

And the way she covertly watched him watching her.

Did he also watch her watch him, watching her?

A delicious little quiver tiptoed up her spine at the idea.

Enough, Celestia scolded herself.

Think of something else lest you make a complete

cake of yourself.

Anything or *anyone* other than the powerful man prowling back and forth, back and forth, mere feet from her. Anything but what it would be like to be under his protection. To know him in the intimate way a man and woman knew one another.

Was it worth her ruination, though?

For the unmitigated truth of it was, a man of his station would never lower himself to marry a commoner. Besides, Landry had never hinted at anything inappropriate between them despite his sizzling glances.

In fact, he'd been aghast when she'd believed he'd improperly propositioned her.

STOP, Celestia Andromeda Josette Tolman.

Just stop, for pity's sake

She scrambled for something else to ponder.

Wyatt Johnson and Nelson Black.

Yes, that would do to distract her errant musings.

The two lads Landry had retained as apprentices had become adept at overseeing the store, and she had become perfectly comfortable leaving the operation in their hands for a few hours. Intelligent and unexpectedly articulate, both young men professed an interest in training as amanuensis as well. Which meant the real possibility that Tolman Tomes—Scrivener and Stationer might actually have a future.

Surprisingly, Uncle Paul had approved of the idea and, beaming, announced his plans to only work two days a week henceforth. Fridays and Saturdays, he instructed Wyatt and Nelson on scribing and shorthand.

Today, only Nelson worked in the store. Wyatt had come down with a vicious cold yesterday, and Celestia, after assuring him his position was not in jeopardy, had sent him home until he was well.

A scowl wrinkled her forehead as she waited for Landry to continue.

Just when she believed finances might be manageable, Uncle Paul had decided to reduce his hours. Not that she blamed him. He was nearing seven-and-sixty, and his health had been failing for years.

She had not mentioned transforming the upper level into living accommodations yet. Not with Papa valiantly trying to remain sober. Their house was situated much farther away from the taverns and pubs that populated many lanes near the bookstore.

After a lengthy, private discussion with Landry that first day he had arrived for transcribing, which Celestia was not privy to, her father had taken himself home. He had not appeared in the shop since, but neither had he, to her knowledge, taken a single swallow of liquor.

To her absolute astonishment, he had begun cooking supper and even tidying up the house.

She had no idea what Landry had said, but whatever it had been, it appeared to have worked. Every day, it was on the tip of her tongue to ask Landry, and every time she quashed the impulse.

He would tell her when he wanted her to know.

Or else Papa would.

She closed her eyes, sending a silent prayer heavenward that, at long last, her father might have put his drinking behind him. The previous three years had been a trial, to be sure, and she honestly had not known how she could go on with things as they were.

"Celestia?"

Landry's warmth beckoned to her from beside her chair. He stood so near that she smelled that combination of him that never failed to unhinge her knees and cause a little flutter in her tummy.

Soap and starch and sandalwood and cloves.

And something woodsy she could not quite put her finger on. Perhaps juniper or eucalyptus or cedar.

Someone really ought to bottle that aroma and call it *Essence of Earl* or *Male Magnetism*.

They'd make a fortune.

"Celestia? Are you all right?"

Worry drove the tenor of Landry's voice an octave lower.

He placed his large palm upon her shoulder. His bare fingers grazed her collarbone, and she all but melted and slid from her chair. Every pore came alive at his touch, and Celestia feared she was on the brink of either disintegrating or erupting into an inferno.

Clothing rustled, and she became aware he had crouched beside her in his concern.

Oh, Lord.

He was so close, and she felt her body sway toward his, the traitorous thing. She was helpless to resist his masculine pull.

"Celestia?"

His fingers tightened the merest bit.

Opening her eyes, she found herself sinking into pools of quicksilver fringed in thick, black lashes. She could not have broken the connection had she wanted to, and God above, she did *not* want to.

Desire flared in Landry's eyes before he boldly

sank his attention to her parted mouth, descending lower to the expanse of feminine flesh her bodice did not conceal, and then returned lazily up her face to meet her eyes again.

A sideways grin tilted his seductive mouth.

He knows.

Indeed, he knew very well how he affected her.

"I very, *very* much want to kiss you, Celestia," Landry's voice emerged as a throaty purr.

Yes. Yes. Yes.

Could he possibly be as overcome as she?

Licking her lips, Celestia struggled to find her voice. To agree without sounding like a wanton hussy or an immoral strumpet. Or utterly desperate.

"May I kiss you?" he asked. "Please?"

Of course, he would not force himself on her. He was a true gentleman in behavior and character. Landry gave her the choice.

She nodded and managed a barely audible, "Please."

11

Keyworth, I heard something disconcerting today from that whoremonger, Thruxby, and wanted to alert you. Unsavory rumors are circulating about your relationship with the children you employ— particularly the boys. Who have you angered of late? Do you know of anyone with a vendetta? I must speak with you at your earliest convenience. Not in public. Come directly to my house.

~Urgent note to the Earl of Keyworth from the Earl of Sharonford

Tolman Tomes—Scrivener and Stationer
Oxford Street, St. Giles, London
A Few Minutes Later

Landry had fought the desire to sweep Celestia into his arms and claim her sweet rosebud mouth for weeks. At this instant, when she gazed at him with such longing in her jade green eyes, even knowing it was foolhardy, he could not resist for another moment.

"Sweet, Celestia," he murmured before gazing his mouth over her silky cheek. Then the other cheek. Then the delicate, fragrant skin between her neck and ear.

She smelled of soap and cinnamon and Celestia.

Her little gasp of pleasure spurred him onward.

It had taken Herculean effort to appear unaffected each time he saw her. To hold his emotions and desire in check for days on end for fear of insulting her and destroying this remarkable, precious thing burgeoning between them.

"Please," she implored again, her voice a breathless whisper as she tilted her mouth up in invitation.

"Kiss me, Landry."

How could he refuse what his heart wanted more than his next breath?

Scooping her into his arms, he cradled her small form against him as he settled his frame into her chair.

Her unsightly plain gowns could not disguise her tantalizing woman's figure, the likes of which he had never beheld. Full, ripe breasts, a small waist that flared into generous hips, which swayed provocatively when she moved.

When Celestia had entered the office today wearing this green gown, almost the same shade as her stunning eyes, it was as if spring had arrived in all of her illustrious glory. The verdant shade brought out the bronze and golden ribbons in Celestia's chestnut hair, and her honey-toned skin glowed with health.

She was, in a word, exquisite.

And hope had ventured to bloom within his chest that she had put aside her drab-colored frocks and dared to wear something bright and colorful because of him. She should always wear color and never hide her beauty under unbecoming sacks again.

Landry would be bound she had deliberately done so to discourage unwanted masculine attention. Regardless, even attired in the dull grays and browns she had favored, she could not disguise her beauty.

No doubt, that is why men had degraded Celestia with their offensive offers.

By God, he *would* have all of their names, and they would know his wrath.

A groan throttled up Landry's throat when she adjusted her position. He had been at half-staff since that day in the bookstore when she'd erroneously believed he had offered to make her his mistress.

Never would he degrade her so.

Not this woman who had come to mean everything to him.

It was not just her beauty, for he knew many women who others would consider more attractive. Neither was it only her keen intelligence or ready wit or her unflappable courage.

In truth, it was all of those things and more. Much, much more.

But he could not simplify what this sentiment was with mere words. They jumbled in his mind and wrapped around his tongue. What he felt for Celestia was beyond words. It kindled joy in his spirit and simultaneously frightened the hell out of him.

Trailing his mouth over her arched neck, Landry delighted in her whimpers and sighs. In the way her hands clutched at his coat and how she instinctively pressed into him.

At last, he could bear it no more, and with tender reverence, he grazed her lips with his own.

Heaven. Bliss. Perfection.

She whimpered and raised her torso upward so that her mouth met his.

Her passion did not surprise him.

In his study, he'd seen a flash of the fiery woman she kept subdued behind her prim and proper exterior. That carefully constructed propriety was a thin shell, a veneer she presented to the world, behind which sizzled a spitfire.

He had every intention of cracking that shell wide

open and allowing the magnificent woman within her freedom. Freedom to be herself and to shine in all of her resplendent glory.

Celestia curled one hand into his hair and parted her mouth at his gentle urging.

Sweeping her tongue with his, primal satisfaction thrummed through Landry's blood. She gasped and eagerly returned the movement. Dueling, lashing, sparring, their tongues mated, their breaths coming in ever-increasing deep rasps.

They needed to stop before this went too far.

He had only intended to kiss her, but he was near to losing control.

He did not lose control.

Reluctantly, Landry lifted his head.

"Darling, we had better stop."

Someone could come upon them at any moment.

Wyatt and Nelson were quick studies, but they poked their heads into the office with a question or three or four every day. Landry would not risk Celestia's reputation or make her tattle fodder for the gossips.

Her eyelids slowly flickered open, and she gave him such a beatific smile, a piece of his heart tumbled to her dainty feet.

"Yes, of course."

With a jerky little nod, she straightened, and he helped her to stand.

He brushed a loose tendril of silky chestnut hair behind her ear. She wore her hair in a Grecian knot today. The softer style flattered her oval face and displayed the luxuriousness of her hair.

Twin spots of color accented her cheeks, but she pinned him with one of her direct looks.

Had he finally found a woman wholly incapable of artifice?

"Thank you," she said softly, diffidently.

"Thank you?" Landry repeated stupidly.

For what?

Kissing her?

Stopping?

What a marvel Celestia Tolman was.

A shy smile bloomed across her radiant face, her lips swollen and berry red from his kisses. She gave a little self-conscious smile and lifted a shoulder as if to say, *I do not know. Do not ask me to explain.*

And he understood, because Landry, too, could not put what had happened between them into words. It was far more than a first kiss, and he would vow she also knew it.

This was love in all of its imperfect, complex, and astonishing glory.

He loved her.

Landry, Earl of Keyworth, loved, adored, cherished Celestia Tolman, prim and proper bluestocking.

She and no other soothed his spirit, calmed his soul, brought him unparalleled peace, and yet stirred his carnal desires into an inferno with an innocent look.

His attention flicked to her new gown.

Or a delectable expanse of velvety flesh above her modest bodice.

All, he had no doubt, without any intention of seduction or allure on her part.

She was, without exception, the most unaffected and unpretentious woman he had ever met. With her, Landry always knew exactly where he stood. He trusted her too, and that was why he now knew unequivocally that she could not have anything to do with the nasty chatter currently circulating about him.

That had not been the case when the *on dit* began weeks ago.

"Do you fear I have a vengeful streak?" she had quipped that day she had asked for his help, and he'd

denied her his aid. Unforgivable of him when she had hinted how desperate her plight was.

In truth, he *had* wondered if she would behave as a woman scorned.

Now, he found the notion wholly untenable. After one day of working with Celestia, Landry dismissed her as the culprit. She was not capable of such premeditated malevolence or of spreading rancorous rumors.

Rumors so disgusting that Sharonford had insisted on meeting Landry at his home rather than at one of their gentlemen's clubs to disclose the exact nature of the gossip.

Someone was very capable, however. And that someone seemed determined to destroy Landry's reputation and political career by spreading tattle that he required sexual favors from the children he hired.

Too deuced bad Britmere was not in London, or he would set the investigator on the rumormonger's trail in short order.

Soon enough, perhaps as early as the day after tomorrow, Britmere would be back with Lenora and Mrs. Smythe—that is Laureen and Mrs. Smith—in tow, if all went as planned. Landry had sent his coach to fetch his sister and her adopted mother. Mrs. Smith would always have a home with him.

After all, without the benefit of a husband and amidst an ugly scandal, she'd raised Lenora. He owed the woman a huge debt of gratitude, and he would see that she lived the remainder of her days in comfort.

Meanwhile, Landry had instructed his staff to not allow any children inside his house or on the grounds. Extra help had been hired to attend the household duties as well as prepare food for the waifs. Meals were dispersed in the alley adjacent to Landry's house, morning and evening.

It had only taken a few days for the urchins to understand the temporary change in their employment. For those who had younger siblings to feed, food was sent home with them. Presently, he did not dare pay them in coin, and he made sure he was never present when the food and other supplies were distributed.

Teeven and Fiske, Landry's valet, had been tasked with overseeing the children's welfare who had been put out of a position, as all depended on the coins they earned.

Familiar anger raised its thorny head, but Landry tamped it down. This was not the time to dwell on such unpleasantness. He shoved that ugly business to a recess of his mind to explore later.

Right now, he had something much more pleasant to ponder.

"I must go below, Landry," Celestia said, indicating the broken pen with a sweeping gesture. "I need a new quill. Give me a moment, please."

"By all means."

It would give him time to wrestle his ardor under control and provide her a few moments to regain her equanimity.

She started to turn away but then glanced at the small clock on the slightly lopsided and cluttered shelf nearby before facing him. "Shall I put water on for tea too?"

"Please."

"I made seed cake this morning." With a nuance of a smile hovering at the corners of her mouth, she left.

Landry had told her seed cake was a particular favorite of his, and the minx had baked it for him.

The days he dictated to her, they shared tea in the afternoon. She always baked a tasty treat or two, and the half-hour or so they spent chatting had become something he eagerly anticipated.

They spoke about all manner of things: their

parents, her brothers and his sister, the places they wanted to visit, his dog, which he assured her was a big, gentle brute, and much more.

He'd learned her dreams—or at least part of them, and he had shared details of himself he'd never revealed to another person. Landry also regaled her with humorous tales of mishaps at balls, musicals, museums, and the theater.

Celestia had laughed until tears trailed down her porcelain cheeks.

She told him of the books she had read, her favorite flower—irises—how she'd always wanted to learn to ride a horse and dreamed of the day when women could openly pursue the same careers as men.

It seems his little bluestocking had read Mary Wollstonecraft's writings. While Celestia did not agree with everything the philosopher wrote, she did very much believe men were not naturally superior to women simply because they were born males.

Landry could not have agreed more.

He supposed it was not precisely proper for them to be alone in the office. Chiefly as neither Celestia's uncle nor father occupied the office next door as he had initially anticipated. That unfortunate circumstance could not have been predicted when he'd retained Celestia's transcribing services, and he sure as hell was not giving her the sack now.

Nonetheless, Landry always left the door wide open and made sure, until today, to dictate from across the room from her. That way, if someone ventured upstairs, they would see nothing worth remarking upon.

Pounding on the stairs had him turning his head before Nelson, red-faced and highly agitated, stumbled to the stop. "My lord, Miss Tolman needs yer assistance straightaway. There is a cove below who won't leave her be. He is behavin' in a most improper fashion."

12

I know it's foolhardy and will undoubtedly result in heartbreak. The instant I admitted to myself that I'd fallen in love with Landry, I should've stopped scribing for him. But what can it hurt? He does not know, and that's the only way I can be with him. I realize he'll have to marry someday and produce an heir. Why shouldn't I claim this time while I can?

~Miss Celestia Tolman to her diary

Tolman Tomes—Scrivener and Stationer
Oxford Street, St. Giles, London
Still 6 May 1818

Landry was out the door before Nelson finished speaking. Taking the stairs two at a time, he raced below. He jumped down the last three, landing with a heavy thud.

"I said release me, Sir Cronk."

Though Celestia's voice was steady, an undercurrent of alarm tinged her words.

"Come now, Celestia," a familiar, irritating male voice crooned. "No need to play the coy vixen with me."

The bloody blighter!

Landry wanted to punch Ignatius Cronk to next December.

"Why else would you be wearing such a charming frock if not to entice us men?" Cronk asked, his tone lecherous and condescending.

Nelson's heavy footfall indicated he had also descended the stairs and awaited Landry's instruction.

"I know how women of your ilk think, my dear. Holding out for a bigger prize." Cronk laughed, an unpleasant, nasally snicker. "I suppose I could offer you one hundred pounds annually in addition to a house. More if you please me, my dove. Let's have a kiss to seal our bargain, shall we?"

By all that was holy, Landry would wring the blackguard's neck before pummeling him. He ground his teeth so hard that if he continued grinding them much longer, they'd be dust. He'd gum his food for the rest of his days.

"Release me," Celestia bit out with undisguised ire.

The sounds of a struggle ensued as Landry rounded the end of a bookshelf.

The tableau before him made him see red, and a growl of pure, animalistic fury escaped his clenched teeth.

I'll kill him.

Celestia struggled to escape a rotund, balding gentleman slathering her face with sloppy, wet kisses while he brazenly pawed her breasts.

"Unhand her this instant," Landry roared, sailing across the remaining distance without consciously moving.

Which side of the gargoyle's face should he smash first?

Or should he pulverize his bulbous nose?

Definitely, the nose, if the red-veined, bulging appendage in the center of Cronk's ugly face could even be called that.

Shock contorted the toad's already unpleasant features before he narrowed his eyes to vengeful slits and roughly yanked Celestia closer.

"She is taken, Keyworth," he sneered, curling his lips into a ghastly smile.

Taken? *Taken?*

By all that was divine. How dare this shriveled scrotum in a suit treat Celestia like she was a hackney or a seat at a card table or a pastry?

"I most definitely am not *taken*, sir."

Celestia jerked her arm free of his grasp and rubbed the reddened imprint of Cronk's fingers clearly displayed on her pale skin.

"And I shall never, ever, under *any* circumstances, agree to be kept by the likes of you," she spat. "I am not, nor will I ever be any man's mistress."

Brava, my brave darling.

Landry grinned, pride beating against his ribcage.

She was magnificent in her fury.

Nelson hovered nearby, one hand in his pocket.

Landry had no doubt whatsoever a deadly blade lay nestled there. You could take a youth off the streets, but it took longer than a few weeks to take the street out of the youth. It was to Nelson's credit he had not used the knife on Cronk already.

He probably would have done if Landry had not been above.

Green eyes blazing, Celestia raised her chin. Defiance and affront radiated off her in tangible waves. "Now leave my establishment and never, *ever* return."

"Did Keyworth make you a better offer?" Cronk demanded, sending a sly sideways glance toward Nelson. "I recently heard you preferred buggering boys, like yonder young chap."

Celestia choked on an appalled gasp. "How dare you?"

"You bloody sod. I'll have yer guts for garters," snarled Nelson, brandishing a lethal-looking stiletto.

Landry raised his hand in a halting gesture.

"Nelson," he ordered with a hint of steel in his voice. "Put the knife away."

Nelson lowered the blade to his side but did not return it to his pocket.

Fair enough.

"I told you to leave." Celestia sent Nelson an anxious glance. "You are not welcome here."

Was she afraid he would attack Cronk?

It was no more than the assling deserved.

Cronk's features contorted in haughty wrath. "You forget whom you address, you little slut…"

Landry leaped forward and planted the wretch a facer. Bone crunched and Cronk howled in pain as he flew backward, crashing into the wall.

"She said to leave, Cronk. I shall give you until the count of three."

He held up three fingers.

Chest heaving, Landry tossed a glance toward the display window. A small, open-mouthed crowd had gathered. Eyes agog, they gawped at the scene playing out within the bookstore.

Better than a Drury Lane tragedy and all for free.

Devil and damn.

The chinwags would be in fine fettle when they caught wind of this.

Cronk dragged a less than clean handkerchief from his pocket and, pressing the stained wad to his damaged nose, attempted to staunch the bleeding.

"You'll pay for this, Keyworth," he mumbled from beneath the cloth.

Landry flicked him a disinterested glance.

"Really, Cronk?"

Twisting his mouth into a derisive smile, Landry shook his head as he reached for Celestia and drew her behind him.

"One." Landry raised his forefinger.

She made no attempt to resist. Instead, her relieved gaze shouted, "Thank you."

"I do not think so. You see, whoremongers such as you prey on those you deem weaker than yourself. You shan't call me out because you are a craven coward, and you know I would easily best you at swords *and* pistols. You would *not* survive," he grated, allowing all of the loathing bubbling inside him to leach into his voice.

"Two." He held up a second finger.

Cronk edged toward the exit, hatred spewing from his bloodshot eyes.

"Before the day is over, I'll swear to everyone who will listen that I have had that whore a hundred times." Cronk stabbed a finger in Celestia's direction. "This pathetic excuse for a bookstore will go bankrupt. I'll see to it. I have already been dropping hints in the right ears."

Ah, so Cronk was responsible for the decline in the store's clientele.

"And she'll soon be spreading her legs for any sot who can spare a thruppence," Cronk spat.

"Bloody, sodding bugger," Nelson swore, advancing a step. He shot Landry a sidelong glance. "Let me carve him up a bit, gov."

Extending his hand, palm outward again, Landry stopped the infuriated lad.

To hell with a count of three.

Instead, Landry prowled forward. Just when Cronk darted for the door, he extended a leg, tripping the spawn of Satan.

As Cronk lay cowering on the floor, Landry

relished the fear in the other man's meaty, sweat-covered face.

"First, *I* have a vested interest in this building. I would not take kindly to you defaming a business within its walls." Landry leaned over, gratified to see terror widening Cronk's cow-manure green eyes. He seized Cronk's bloodied neckcloth and jerked him upward.

"Secondly, you worthless piece of excrement, Celestia Tolman will soon be the Countess of Keyworth. I *shall* call *you* out and end your miserable life if you besmirch her in any way whatsoever. What's more, the *ton* will applaud me for ridding their number of a detested scourge like you."

I cannot believe it, though Mama assures me it is so! I have a brother, and he is an earl! An earl, of all things. Mama says my given name is Lenora. However, she and Papa changed it when I came to live with them. Tomorrow, we travel to London to meet the Earl of Keyworth. That is, Landry, my brother. He sent his coach for us to make use of. I do hope he is a good person. He would not have been looking for me for eight years if he were not, would he?

~Miss ~~Laureen Smythe~~ Lenora Audsley to her diary

Tolman Tomes—Scrivener and Stationer
Oxford Street, St. Giles, London
Several Chaotic Minutes Later

After Cronk dragged his despicable presence from the store, still swearing vilely beneath his breath, Celestia stood motionless as Landry shooed the riveted onlookers away from the window.

He'd been magnificent in his defense of her. Despite the shock she had just endured, a little thrill zipped through her. Cronk had not stood a sugar lump's chance in hot tea against Landry's wrath and superior strength and intellect.

Even now, he handled the crowd with enviable diplomacy.

She had no doubt that he was a spectacular orator in Parliament.

"I do beg your pardon," Landry said to the onlookers, every bit the self-possessed and polished aristocrat now. He straightened his jacket before arranging his features in an estimable semblance of penance and stately pride.

"I regret you witnessed my less than gentlemanly behavior. However, I had no choice but to defend my betrothed's honor after Mr. Cronk put his hands upon her person and disparaged her character."

Why did he keep saying that?

They assuredly were not betrothed as much as Celestia wished with all of her heart otherwise.

The *on dit* would already be horrendous without adding a false betrothal to the inferno.

In point of fact, Tolman Tomes—Scrivener and Stationer might very well be further shunned after this debacle. Which, once again, was none of her doing but which she would bear the brunt of.

Blast Ingantius Cronk to Hades.

God, then what would Celestia do?

"Served him right, the bugger," one skinny man wearing a tweed suit said, scratching his temple.

"I should say so," a stout woman attired in a godawful chartreuse and orange walking costume agreed while enthusiastically brandishing her cane. "Miss Tolman is a proper young miss, she is."

Celestia did not recognize the dame.

A previous customer, perhaps?

"My felicitations, my lord," simpered a pinch-faced, elegantly dressed woman while inspecting Celestia with her critical gaze through the window. "This is the first I have heard of your upcoming nuptials," she said, her shrill voice scraping across Celestia's nerves like a fork on a plate. "There's been no announcement in the news sheets."

She curved her mouth into what Celestia thought was meant to be a smile, but which looked as if she struggled not to pass wind.

"Will the banns be read soon?" she asked in that tinny tone, somewhere between a kettle whistling and a donkey braying. Bold as brass, poking her long nose where it had no business.

No, they most certainly will not!

A shadow flickered across Landry's face, sharpening the already chiseled contours. He did not like this woman.

"Lady Crustworth," he replied with the meagerest downward angle of his strong square chin.

It did not escape Celestia that he had not answered the busybody's question.

Who was this Lady Crustworth?

She had never been inside the shop, of that Celestia was positive.

Disapproval etched every crease of the woman's haughty face as she regarded Celestia through the storefront glass.

Celestia would've remembered her. Would've recalled her disdain.

One tended to do that when one encountered someone who loathed you on sight.

Landry did not appear any too pleased to see the lady either.

Sweeping a hand through his tousled hair, he passed his gaze over the crowd. "You may go about your business now. All is well."

"Not for the gent ye sent on his way, it ain't," a rough-looking character missing a front tooth and needing a shave chortled, slapping his thigh.

A few others joined in his laughter.

Not, however, Lady Crustworth.

If anything, her mouth pursed tighter.

Spying someone across the street, she lifted her

hand, calling in a sing-song voice, "Sylvia. *Yoo-hoo.* Sylvia Darumple! Do wait for me."

Sylvia Darumple and her miserable-countenanced maid came to a stop. They peered inquisitively at the matron scurrying toward them with notable alacrity for a person of her age and lack of decorum for one of her lofty station.

Shoes clacking loudly on the pavement, Lady Crustworth bustled away. "Sylvia, you simply will not believe what…"

A passing carriage drowned out the rest of her words, but Celestia could guess what they were. She'd be bound the telling did not spin her in a flattering light.

Shivering and hugging herself, she could not seem to move her leaden feet. They were anchored in place. She ought to remove herself from the gawking bystanders' curious perusal, but every bit of energy seemed to have seeped from her.

For the first time in her three-and-twenty years, she feared she might faint.

Her mind kept replaying Cronk's assault—his groping hands and revolting mouth. What he'd accused Landry of—improper relations with boys—was the crudest, most grotesque accusation.

Were people really saying those vile things about Landry?

Nausea billowed up her throat, hot and acrid.

She swallowed once. Twice. And a third time.

No, she would not faint, but she might well cast up her accounts.

"Are you all right?" Landry's tender inquiry as he touched her upper arm brought her back to herself, and she nodded, sliding a glance to the window.

The crowd had finally disbursed, thank God.

"Yes. Yes, I am fine."

She was not, but not for the reasons Landry no doubt believed had shaken her to her very core.

"Here, Miss Tolman."

Worry crinkling his forehead, Nelson handed Celestia her shawl. It must've slipped from her shoulders during her struggle with Cronk.

"Thank you, Nelson. You were wise to fetch his lordship."

Flushing, he nodded, his mouth pulled into a taut line as he slid Landry a knowing look. "I still wish ye'd let me cut him, my lord. His kind only understands that sort of talk."

Celestia suspected Nelson might be correct in that regard. However, if he had laid even a finger on Cronk, the youth would've faced severe charges. Cronk might be scum, but he was noble scum, and current laws protected aristocrats.

Why wouldn't they?

The elites created the laws, which always seemed to benefit them at the common man's expense.

"My lord, may I have a word with you upstairs?" She met Landry's concerned gaze, unable to keep the accusation out of hers.

If she'd heard him correctly in her distress, he had claimed an interest in the bookshop building.

An interest.

What exactly did that mean?

Did that mean he'd somehow purchased their building out from under them?

How? When? Why?

It made no sense.

Of more import, what did he think he was doing by announcing to the world that she was his betrothed?

Dear God. Her stomach cramped. Surely he knew he could not make such a claim and then retract his statement later? People would assume all sorts of sordid things.

Celestia would be utterly ruined. Not in the manner a debutante or lady of society was ruined, but disgraced nonetheless.

Until he had throttled Cronk, she had not thought Landry impulsive. But perhaps all that riled up male virility or his manly ego had prompted him to blurt that she was his betrothed. Or mayhap, he'd simply called upon the most effective and useful means to shut Ignatius Cronk's vulgar mouth.

"Now is not the time, Celestia," Landry said. "I know you have many questions, and I shall be happy to answer them tomorrow evening."

What?

Tomorrow evening?

Celestia was not waiting until tomorrow to have this discussion.

Suppressing the impulse to stamp her foot and shout at him like a retractable child, she forced calm into her voice.

"That is unacceptable, my lord."

Sighing, Landry slid a troubled glance toward the street. "I do not trust Cronk to keep his mouth shut, Celestia. Or Lady Crustworth, for that matter. She's one of the *ton's* worst chinwags, as is Sylvia Darumple."

Of course, they were.

"I must deflect as much damage as I can as soon as possible, Celestia. There is no time to spare," Landry said, the corner of his eyes crinkling.

"Oh." She deflated like a fireplace bellow.

He was not trying to avoid the conversation.

Once again, his purpose was to protect her.

"You have had a terrible shock, my dear." Cupping

her shoulders gently as he peered into her eyes, he said, "Go home. Nelson will escort you. I beg you. Stay there so that I'll know you are safe. Do not open the shop tomorrow."

Celestia jerked her head up.

"Not open? But, Landry, I cannot afford to keep the doors closed for even a day," she protested.

Pride be hanged.

Pride did not pay the mortgage or put food on the table.

He gave her a boyish smile and grazed her cheek with his bent forefinger.

As was becoming a habit, her blood hummed in her veins at his touch.

"You need not carry that burden alone any longer."

She had no idea what he meant by that and was convinced he would not explain himself now either.

"But won't keeping the store closed cause more gossip?" she asked instead.

Naturally, it would. Conjecture and speculation would fly about London like dandelion down in a meadow on a blustery day.

"I have a plan, but I cannot take the time to explain everything right now. I need you to trust me, Celestia." Landry tilted her chin upward, his gaze tender and caressing. "Can you do that?"

She searched his face, and what she saw shimmering in his eyes stalled her breath.

Yes. Yes, I would do anything for you.

His mouth curled into a confident rogue's smile, and a knowing glint lit his gray eyes. For a mortifying instant, Celestia panicked, thinking she'd spoken aloud.

Had she?

"I shall call at your home tomorrow evening and have a discussion with your father and uncle. I'll send a missive, so they expect me. All will be well, Tia, I promise."

He had remembered her brothers' pet name for her. She had shared that personal detail during tea last week.

What morsel of her heart Landry had not already claimed became his at that moment.

Acutely aware, Nelson stood but a few feet away and avidly took in all that transpired. Celestia caught the corner of her lower lip between her teeth.

All would *not* be well. Not by half.

Landry must know that also and was trying to alleviate her qualms.

Arguing would serve no purpose because he was right. He stood a far greater chance of squelching the gossip than she could ever hope to. She mightn't want to, but she could wait until tomorrow to speak with him.

What reason would she give Papa and Uncle for

being home earlier than usual?

A version of the truth.

Just enough to pacify their curiosity—not a whisper about that nonsensical betrothal business.

Facing Nelson, Landry withdrew his purse from his inside coat pocket. He passed the youth several coins. "Hail a hackney, Nelson. I'd like you to accompany Miss Tolman to her home. You may ride atop with the jarvey. There is enough money to take a hack home yourself too."

"Yes, sir." Nelson bobbed his head and darted for the door.

"I'll fetch my cloak and bonnet." Celestia needed a few minutes to collect herself.

What did Landry think Cronk would do?

Follow her home?

She shuddered at the rather petrifying idea as she collected her belongings. After shrugging into her coat and tying her plain black bonnet's ribbons, she returned to the front of the store.

Landry stood, one shoulder propped against a bookshelf, gazing out the window. At her approach, he turned. He regarded her so soberly, with such intensity, she braced herself for what she knew was coming.

The retraction of his claim that they were affianced.

He must've decided not to wait until tomorrow

then. Just as well. Better to get it over and done with.

"Celestia?"

She would save him the trouble. Likely as not, Cronk would sully her reputation beyond redemption anyway. At least she could spare Landry the awkwardness of calling off a false betrothal.

"My lord, you need not remark upon the matter." The "my lord" was for her benefit. To remind her of her station and the great chasm of class difference that separated them. She ought never to have allowed her emotions free reign. "I certainly did not take your claim of our betrothal serious."

"What if *I* did?"

14

Mama, I have met the most extraordinary woman.
You would adore her, I think. She's not a noblewoman,
but I believe you, of all people, would understand.
Love does not recognize birth or position, nor
power or prestige. I vowed on your deathbed that I'd
find my sister. That same night, I promised myself
I would marry a commoner if she loved me and I
loved her. As it happens, Lenora has been found,
Mama. What is more, I have fallen in love.
I want to spend the rest of my life with Celestia.

~Letter from Landry, Earl of Keyworth, to the
deceased Countess of Keyworth.
Torn up and burned

Tolman Residence
Number 36 Carnaby Street, London
7 May 1818—Evening

*W*hat if I did? What if I did? What if I did?*
The dratted refrain played over and over in Celestia's mind. A preposterous mantra that would not cease, though she had repeatedly ordered the monologue to hush since yesterday. Honestly, she did

not know what to make of Landry's flummoxing declaration.

One minute her hope soared skyward like an eagle and the next plummeted like raging water over rocky falls.

Before she could respond or ask Landry precisely what he meant, Nelson had poked his head in the door—his timing utterly, utterly abhorrent.

"The hackney is waitin', my lord."

Landry had unceremoniously bundled her inside the musty-smelling conveyance, and with a softly murmured, "Please do not leave your house tomorrow," had shut the door and signaled the driver.

Now, the fire played shadows over his handsome features as he lounged in a saggy-cushioned armchair, all lean masculine grace, chatting amicably with Papa and Uncle Paul about horses, politics, tobacco, and sheep.

Sheep, of all things.

What did Papa or Uncle Paul know about sheep other than they produced wool and mutton?

Celestia, on the other hand, knew more about the creatures than either of them. Nevertheless, she must smile politely and pretend ignorance.

Early in her teens, she had gone through a phase

where she was fascinated with barnyard animals and read everything she could get her hands on about them. *That* knowledge was not something a bluestocking shared willingly unless they wished others to stare as if one was an oddity displayed at Bullock's Museum.

For instance, sheep pupils were rectangular, and they could see behind themselves. Oh, and breeding sheep was referred to as tupping, which strangely, was a term Madame Bonacieux had also mentioned in her memoir.

Along with rogering, swiving, and shagging.

All crude words to describe copulating.

Something else Celestia was not supposed to know *anything* about.

After transcribing the madame's memoirs, she possessed carnal knowledge that would send most well-bred ladies into a swoon.

Heat stung her cheeks. She pointed her attention to her plain black half-boots peeking from the hem of her blue gown. She'd donned the remade frock to boost her confidence.

Oh, very well.

Celestia allowed she had worn the pretty gown because she wanted to look attractive.

Only she did not own any silken slippers and had to wear her sensible boots. Until recently, she had not cared a whit about their ugliness. Her footwear was practical and durable. Now she found herself longing for pretty, impractical beaded silk slippers and stockings embroidered with flowers and garlands.

Glancing up, she caught Landry's bold, appreciative perusal from beneath his hooded lids. Not for the first time since his arrival either.

A secret thrill fluttered around her heart.

Celestia Tolman will soon be the Countess of Keyworth.

I had no choice but to defend my betrothed's honor. What if I did?

Botheration!

Would her errant thoughts never stop tormenting and taunting her?

No, because Landry owned her heart—every last tiny piece of it.

Every time they were together, another part had become his. Lord knew Celestia had not wanted to fall in love with him. She had doggedly determined to guard her emotions and heart against his charisma and charm.

That disarming tilt of his sculpted mouth and the

glow in his striking gray eyes.

At this very moment, a shock of hair hung over his forehead, adding to his devil-may-care rakishness.

A beeswax taper held over a flame was made of stiffer stuff than she when it came to Landry. A single glance from his smoldering eyes or a roguish tilt of his mouth, and she all but melted.

God help her, but she was well on to becoming a calf-eyed ninny.

Compelling her lips to bend upward a fraction more, Celestia forced herself to look away. Her jaw ached from the false smile she had pasted upon her face three-quarters of an hour ago when Landry had arrived. If she kept this pretense up much longer, would her face actually crack?

It certainly felt as if it would.

Initially, she had busied herself with tea pouring and serving the biscuits and cakes she'd made earlier in the day. The Tolmans might not have much compared to the upper ten thousand, but Celestia could present a tea tray and dainties that would not shame them.

Papa and Uncle Paul were pleased as Punch that a peer had graced their home. The note Landry had sent around earlier said he wished to discuss a business venture with them and would call this evening at half of seven.

Did this business undertaking have anything to do with his claim of a vested interest in the building?

Celestia bit her tongue and curled her toes tight in her boots to keep from informing Papa and Uncle that the earl was not there to just see them. He had a matter of some import to discuss with her as well.

Of course, she realized how special an occasion this was—to have a member of *le beau monde* sipping tea in their parlor. A first and likely last occurrence. It was one thing for Papa to visit the earl's residence as his scrivener and another entirely to have that same noble take tea with them.

On the other hand, she had become so accustomed to Landry's presence that she sometimes forgot he was a noble. Probably because he never behaved like a pretentious, self-important peer of the realm. Not even that day when she'd sneaked into his house. She'd been able to speak to him freely, and he had not acted the least condescending or autocratic.

A wonder, too, that Papa and Landry seemed on quite cordial terms. One wouldn't have thought that would be the case, considering the earl had sacked her father. What was more, Landry had insisted on having a delicate conversation with Papa about his over-imbibing.

Nonetheless, although every sense was keenly alert, Celestia could not detect an undercurrent of hostility or resentment between the earl and her father.

Her father and uncle acted the proud hosts while she sat on the green and yellow floral chintz sofa, very much aware of how outdated and worn the furnishings in their comfortable home were. The cozy house that they might need to sell to save their business.

That conversation was long overdue, but in light of what had happened yesterday, she was unsure if it made any difference now. Perhaps she might impose upon Landry's duchess friends to write her letters of reference, and Celestia could become a governess.

No, that was not a solution either. She could not earn enough as a governess to provide for Papa and Uncle Paul.

Rather than ruminate on that troublesome subject, she turned her attention once more to their guest, wholly at ease in the overstuffed chair the earl relaxed in. Landry's seat and a matching armchair sat at right angles to the fireplace. Legs crossed, Papa occupied the second chair while Uncle Paul sat on the far side of the sofa from Celestia.

The lumpy sofa paralleled the hearth, and a rather battered Chinese Ming Square coffee table sat centered between the chairs and sofa. Candles glowed in a pair of crystal hurricane lamps, one of Mama's greatest treasures, atop the mirrored oak inlaid fireplace mantel.

The green Aubusson rug's frayed edge abutted the hearth's cracked tiles, and a flush of embarrassment heated Celestia. She pointedly kept her attention focused on the small fire cavorting behind the sooty screen.

Had she not been in Landry's elegant townhome, she would never have felt self-conscious about her residence. To be fair, he did not appear to look down his nose at their much humbler dwelling. But then, he would not, would he?

She shifted her regard to him once more. Something she couldn't seem to help. Landry drew her gaze to him like the proverbial moth to a flame.

It was not in his nature to act superior or condescending. Not for a man who readily employed street ragamuffins.

Papa sat a little straighter, and after sending

Celestia a doting glance, cleared his throat. "I understand there was a bit of a dust-up at the shop yesterday, my lord."

Landry lifted that dratted dark eyebrow and settled his beautiful gaze upon Celestia.

She heard his silent question as clearly as if he'd asked it in those clipped, upper-class tenors.

"What precisely did you tell them?"

15

I saw the skirmish myself—saw Keyworth bloody Cronk's nose. I also heard the earl claim that common chit was his betrothed with my own ears. What is this world coming to when a prize catch on the Marriage Mart settles for a common shop girl? I, for one, do not believe Keyworth. He's a sentimental do-gooder. Always going on and on about orphans, ragamuffins, and other riff-raff. He won't marry the lowborn gel. That Tolman wench is too far beneath him.

~Letter from Lady Crustworth to Lady Clutterbuck

Tolman Residence
Number 36 Carnaby Street, London
That Same Evening

*O*h, no, Landry, you did not. Celestia told him as much with her slightly narrowed gaze.

They were not going to discuss the debacle with Lord Ignatius Crocodile Cronk until Landry had explained the other matter that had plagued her since yesterday.

Not the betrothal issue.

That required privacy and should take place between the two of them.

Regardless, she would have an answer about his claim of an interest in Tolman Tomes—Scrivener and Stationer's building.

Fashioning her sweetest smile, she blinked innocently.

"My lord, yesterday, you said that you had an interest in Tolman Tomes—Scrivener and Stationer's building?" Celestia placed her cooled tea on the table and schooled her features into a benign expression. "Would you care to elaborate? I am sure we would all like to know to what you referred."

She included her father and uncle in the query. Surely they were as curious as she.

Landry chuckled, then kicked his mouth into a broad grin. "I have purchased the building to the right of Tolman Tomes—Scrivener and Stationer. I'd also like to purchase your building and, if you are agreeable, move your shop to another location I own on Bond Street."

Papa and Uncle Paul exchanged flabbergasted glances.

"Bond Street, you say?" Uncle Paul said, obviously enthusiastic about the notion. "That would be quite,

quite exceptional."

Bond Street was a highly coveted venue for any merchant, the Tolmans included. It was also *very* expensive. Well beyond their means, in point of fact.

Rubbing his chin, Papa nodded slowly. "What are your plans for the other buildings?"

A grin lit Landry's face, and his eyes snapped with excitement. "I would like to turn the upper floors into housing for street youths—one for girls and the other for boys. Naturally, I would also retain an adult to supervise the children and a cook for each establishment. The lower level would host a business or businesses that would provide professional training for those same youths."

Chagrin swept Celestia, quickly followed by admiration. She'd been worried Landry's motives were far less altruistic.

Did he ever do anything for selfish reasons?

No, not since she'd known him.

Fingers steepled on his slightly paunchy belly, Uncle Paul chuckled. "I have no objection. In fact, I think it is a capital idea. Jonathan? Celestia?"

Bless him for including her in the decision. Few men would have done.

"I'd like to see the Bond Street building first, if I may. However, if it proves satisfactory, I think it a brilliant notion too." Papa lifted his teacup toward Landry as if it were a glass of spirit in a silent salute.

No. No. *No.*

What were they thinking?

Their present building was almost paid for.

Real estate on Bond Street was at a premium, costing three or four times what they'd paid for the current location. They would never be able to afford a building there, even if it had a habitable upper level. Which Celestia very much doubted. At least not one large enough for three people to live comfortably.

Was she the only one in their family who considered every aspect of Landry's suggestion before eagerly jumping from the pan into the proverbial fire?

Landry's quicksilver gaze bored into her. "What do you think, Celestia?"

Again, he crossed the mark using her given name.

Why did she have the distinct impression his question comprised more than her approval regarding a new location for Tolman Tomes—Scrivener and Stationer?

"I think," she said, choosing her words with care, "that there are several important factors that need careful considering before a final decision is made."

"That's my girl." Papa beamed, a smile crinkling his face. "Neither of my sons has a lick of business sense, but Celestia? She is just like her mother. Keen mind and sharp wits. Logical and sensible."

Why didn't the heartfelt compliment fill her with joy?

For heaven's sake. Celestia had never craved flattery, flowery accolades, or platitudes before.

"Aye, she's a credit to her sex," Uncle agreed with a jolly wink.

"She is, indeed." An undercurrent in Landry's smooth-as-velvet timbre made her skin tingle all over. "As reluctant as I am to bring up the unfortunate occurrence yesterday, I believe we must address it," he continued, his timbre taking on a more business-like tone.

"Yes, yes," Papa agreed. "Celestia explained Mr. Cronk made a nuisance of himself, and you encouraged him to leave the shop, your lordship. Please accept my sincerest gratitude for your intervention."

Celestia wetted her lower lip, disinclined to meet Landry's gaze. Simply put, she had downplayed the event, loath to relive the trauma or reveal to her father the exact nature of what had transpired. She had been on pins and needles all day, wondering what slanderous chatter was spreading around London about her and Landry.

Though she told herself she should not care, she

did.

Not just for her sake, but for her father and uncle. For Nelson and Wyatt too. It went without mentioning that she was also severely troubled on Landry's behalf. The repugnant slur Cronk cast on his character was damning.

How could anyone believe Landry capable of such depravity?

Who would propagate such disgusting rumors?

An enemy?

Yes, that made the most sense.

Unfolding his legs, Landry pulled a cuff of his black jacket into place before giving Celestia a speaking glance. His indigo blue and silver paisley waistcoat were the only detraction from his somber attire other than his blindingly white shirt. Even his intricately knotted cravat was comprised of ebony silk.

Trust me, his calm gaze said.

It rattled and exhilarated her that she could so easily read his thoughts and that he could do the same to her.

"Celestia has been tactful in her description," Landry said, idly roving his attention around the parlor before bringing it to rest on Papa.

Her father's and uncles' grizzled eyebrows climbed their identical foreheads at Landry's use of her given name. *Again.* The air fairly crackled with their unspoken questions.

Why did his lordship take such liberties, and dare they remind him—a lord—that he overstepped the bounds?

However, Landry seemed not to notice. Or if he did, he disregarded their unspoken question.

He leaned forward, his jaw hard and expression earnest.

"Cronk set his hands upon your daughter, Mr. Tolman. In full view of several witnesses," Landry clarified. "He also insulted her character, threatened her, and made such a lewd and vulgar proposition, I cannot repeat it."

"By Jove, he did not!" Papa thundered, like the Papa of old.

The sober Papa she'd known before Mama's death. The father who'd protected her and guarded her against the ugliness of the world. Who had praised her intellect and bluestocking tendencies.

"Indeed, sir, he did. I planted him a facer in defense of Celestia's honor."

"You broke his nose," Celestia reminded him, then jutted her chin upward. "Lord or not, that blighter deserved it."

Papa turned a wounded, accusing gaze upon her.

"Why did you not tell me the whole of it, dear girl?"

Forehead puckered, he shook his head and tapped his chin with his forefinger. "This does present a rather difficult conundrum. I do not see how you can continue to work at the store in light of this."

Swallowing her immediate, strong objection, Celestia tried reasoning with him first. "Papa, Nelson and Wyatt are there, as is Lord Keyworth three afternoons a week. I am rarely alone anymore."

If Uncle Paul worked his reduced schedule and Papa began transcribing again, she might never need to be alone in the bookshop.

"'Tis more than that, Celestia," Uncle Paul put in, concern wrinkling the corners of his eyes and downturned mouth. "That blackguard's behavior will have made you a target for all manner of degenerates and curs. I imagine tattle is already being bandied about."

Well, of course it was. But if people hid away whenever the chinwags flapped their tongues, nothing would ever get done.

Uncle sent Landry an apologetic glance. "Whenever a peer is involved in a scandal, the gossip seems particularly fervent."

That was *all* of the time.

Aye, like maggots to manure.

Rakehells and rogues abounded in the peerage.

Even a bluestocking working in a used bookstore had access to the previous weeks' gossip rags and scandal sheets.

Nonetheless, Celestia's stomach sank like a brick in a deep well.

She had mistakenly believed her father and uncle were oblivious to society's goings-on.

"Indeed, sir, it is," Landry said with his usual confidence. "Nonetheless, I have been able to squelch a large degree of the chatter."

"How so, your lordship?" Papa asked, his face folding with confusion, even as hope and gratitude infused his gaze.

Celestia would very much like to know the answer herself.

Landry rose and crossed to her.

Her hands grew clammy as she tipped her head.

What was he about?

Oh. Oh. *Oh*!

Suddenly she knew, absolutely *knew*, and was at once overcome and appalled. Excited and terrified.

He would not.

Not here in front of Papa and Uncle.

Not without speaking to her first.

Not without asking Papa for her hand.

Did she want him to ask Papa for her hand?

No. Yes. No.

Yes?

Dear God. Yes.

Her blood pounded in her ears, and her heart hammered so hard behind her breastbone that she felt it might break free of its confines.

Smiling a rather wicked, enigmatic smile, Landry drew her to her feet by both hands but did not release her at once.

"Landry, you cannot." She shook her head, casting her astonished father a hurried glance.

Drat, she had addressed Landry by his given name in front of her father and uncle.

Still grinning like a cat in the cream, Landry slid an arm about her waist and turned her so that they faced Papa.

"Sir, I love your daughter and, with your blessing, wish to make her my wife as soon as possible."

*I have found the source of the unsavory gossip:
One Lord Wilfred Thruxby, a former client of Madame
Meriette Bonacieux. She gave Thruxby the speech you
wrote about personally helping homeless urchins.
However, Thruxby recently gave Madame Bonacieux her
congé, and the woman is bent on retaliation. She is quite
willing to aid you should you require her assistance. Let
me know how I may be of further service.*

*~Letter to the Earl of Keyworth from Marshall
Britmere, investigator*

*Tolman Residence
Number 36 Carnaby Street, London
An Hour into Lord Keyworth's Visit*

A deafening quiet descended upon the salon for several seconds after Landry's confession. Only the scarlet and yellow-orange fire crackling and snapping in the hearth broke the stillness.

Devil a bit.

"Well, did not expect that. No, I did not," one of the two other men mumbled to fill the awkward chasm.

Landry was not sure which because his attention remained fixed on Celestia's flabbergasted features.

He had not meant to blurt the confession like an uncouth bumbler. In fact, he'd practiced any number of ways in which he planned to tell Celestia he loved her and to ask for her hand in marriage.

In truth, he'd prepared to counter every argument she presented as to why they could not wed. If she chose that route, which of course, he prayed she would not.

By rights, if he were to go about it the correct way, he ought to have met with her father in advance, stated his intentions, and asked for Celestia's hand.

However, Celestia was not a conventional woman.

The truth of it was, Landry rather thought she'd want to be the first to know his feelings and intentions. As luck would have it, his skill for public speeches completely deserted him, and he'd simply spouted the first thing that popped to mind.

Taking in her beloved face, he could not help but grin.

"Surprised you, did I?" he asked.

Her eyes, huge, green, wide and wondering pools, stared up at him, and her pretty rosebud mouth formed a perfect "O" of amazement.

"You love me?" she whispered, her voice so soft and irregular that even standing beside her, he strained to hear the barely audible question.

Leaning nearer, he spoke into her shell-like ear.

"I do, my darling. So very, very much."

Her fragrance wafted upward from her warm skin, an intoxicating feminine aroma.

A loud, gravelly throat-clearing pulled his attention to the two elderly men watching the scene with enthusiastic interest.

"Paul, I could use your assistance with…a…with the…a thingamabob in the kitchen," Jonathan Tolman mumbled, giving his brother a speaking look, which fairly screamed, "Let us leave the lovebirds alone."

Perhaps denser than he appeared, Paul Tolman peered at his younger brother as if the man had two noses or another head.

"*Thingamabob? Kitchen?*" he parroted, his stupefied gaze veering back and forth from Landry and Celestia to his brother.

"Yes, yes." Nodded Jonathan eagerly as he gained his feet. "*You know*, Paul. That whatchamacallit doohickey that arrived yesterday."

Comprehension finally dawned, and Paul Tolman's

countenance lit up like a chandelier.

God above. Landry rolled his eyes ceilingward

The men were as subtle as intoxicated Covent Garden harlots.

"Ah yes. That doodad contraption for…making…ah…butter," Paul said, rising from his chair as well.

Celestia giggled before slapping a palm across her mouth.

In short order, her father and uncle made their way to the door.

His hand upon the lever, Jonathan Toman faced them. "You have my heartfelt blessing."

Landry had fretted Jonathan might hold a grudge because he had dispensed with his service and then took it upon himself to have a frank discussion about what his drinking was doing to his daughter and their business.

Thank goodness, Jonathan Tolman was a reasonable man when sober.

The door closed with a soft *snick*.

Landry turned Celestia toward him, wrapping one arm about her trim waist and cupping her chin with his other hand.

"Please forgive my less than finesse proposal. I had intended to get down on one knee and present you with a ring. I even memorized a rather good speech, if I do say so myself, detailing why we'd make a brilliant match."

Eyes glowing and a smile teasing the edges of her mouth, she tilted her head back. "You were so confident I'd accept?"

"No, actually." He shook his head, then brushed the hair that had fallen over his forehead back with a sweep of his hand. "I fully expected you to present a long, logical list of reasons why you could not."

Two lines creased Celestia's forehead as she scrunched her nose. The mantel clock struck the hour, chiming eight times.

"I am not countess material, Landry. We both know that. I am a commoner and an unapologetic bluestocking. I have no dowry, and I'll never be any good at hostessing house parties, balls, routs, and the like. Your friends will say you have gone mad."

"Mad in love."

Cupping her chin, Landry brushed his lips across her velvety soft mouth.

"I do not give a beggar's purse about any of those

things, my darling. When my mother lay dying and confessed that she had loved a man other than my father and that she had born that man a child, I vowed to myself I would marry a commoner if I loved her and she loved me. Because nothing, absolutely *nothing,* is more important to me than love."

He tasted her sweet mouth again.

"You truly do not care?" she asked.

Her gaze searched his face with such gravity that Landry wanted to capture her mouth with his and prove how very much he didn't give ten damns.

"Your peers will never accept me, Landry."

A half-apologetic, half-defiant smile slanted her pretty lips upward. "I shan't accept being banished to a country estate while you romp around London."

"Romp?" he teased, waggling his eyebrows.

She raised her eyebrows archly.

"Well, whatever it is, reformed rapscallions do when their wives are not about. Need I remind you that I transcribed Madame Bonacieux's memoirs? I recognized several names within those pages." Celestia giggled again. "She really was quite horrid at disguising her ... erm ... *clients.* I cannot but wonder if she did not do so purposefully."

"I definitely have not forgotten," he purred, lowering his voice to a seductive timbre. "In fact, I'd be very curious to know just what you learned while transcribing the madame's memoir."

"Naughty man," Celestia chastised as she turned an adorable shade of pink.

"Not as naughty as I'd like to be." Landry pulled her close. "Say you love me too. Make me the happiest, luckiest man to have ever drawn a breath and agree to be my wife."

Tears sparkled in her eyes. Laying a palm upon his cheek, she smiled.

"I love you too, Landry. And yes. I shall gladly become your wife."

"Tomorrow?" He nuzzled her ear, then whispered, "I have a special license."

Laughing, she stood on her toes and clasped the back of his neck, bringing his mouth down to meet hers. "Yes, my love, tomorrow."

Epilogue

I am the Countess of Keyworth now.
I do not need to confess my dreams or sorrows
between the pages of this journal any longer.
I have my beloved husband with whom I can share
everything, and Lenora has become a dear friend
and confidant too. My life is full and blessed.

The new Countess of Keyworth to her diary—last entry

Faringcroft Park — Earl of Keyworth's Country Seat
Lancaster, England
28 August 1818 – Mid-Morning

"We were supposed to be working on my correspondence to Lord Livingston, Countess."

Giving him a coy look, she raked her gaze over her husband. "You are the one who professed it was too warm and started disrobing."

He possessed the most divine male body, and the crisp dark hair that covered his legs, chest, and arms felt utterly delicious rasping against her own soft flesh.

They'd come to the folly to escape the study's heat.

As often happened, Celestia and Landry ended up making love.

Not that she was complaining.

Instead of returning to her cushioned seat, she collected her fan and wandered to look out over the pond. Swans and ducks glided across the still-as-glass surface. Unfurling her hand-painted lace fan, she leaned against the marble.

Beyond the pond, Lenora and her mother walked arm in arm across the greens.

"I am so delighted you found Lenora, Landry. She is the sister I never had."

Landry came up behind Celestia, wrapping his arms about her waist, and rested his chin upon her head. "Ruth is a treasure too. She's near the same age my mother would've been had she lived. She hasn't begrudged Lenora wanting to use her given name either."

Sighing in contentment, Celestia leaned back into her husband. "I fear we'll have our hands full next season when Lenora makes her Come Out. She's a diamond of the first water if there ever was one."

"Aye, she's incomparable, but I prefer brunettes with green eyes." He nipped her ear, and she giggled.

A stunning redhead with turquoise-blue eyes, Lenora possessed a rare combination of outward and inward beauty.

"Well, at least we do not have to worry about lechers such as Cronk or Thruxby setting their sights on her," Landry said. "Cronk took my advice and found himself an on-the-shelf spinster with a heavy purse and retired to the country."

Which was to say, Landry had told him if he ever saw his face again or even heard a whisper that he was in London, he'd challenge him to an affair of honor.

The idiot had indeed been stupid enough to speak ill of Celestia, and once she became the Countess of Keyworth, Landry had given Cronk two choices: leave London and never return or die on the field of honor.

Cronk had scuttled away so quickly his shadow could not keep up with him.

Due to the diligence of Marshall Britmere, Thruxby had been exposed as a pedophile.

Interesting how those committing crimes so often projected their sins onto others.

Thruxby had despised Landry and his determination to aid London's street children. The degenerate and others of his ilk preyed on those same innocents, finding them easy targets for their depraved appetites.

"I had a letter from Papa today," Celestia said, running her fingertips over the knuckles of Landry's hand at her waist. "Nash has decided to leave the navy and take on overseeing Tolman Tomes and Tobacco." She shook her head. "I honestly never thought the day would come that either of my brothers would willingly leave the sea. Especially to run the shop."

"I am glad Nash wants to enter the family business," Landry murmured into her hair. "Your uncle is getting too old to work, and although your father has given up spirits, he too told me he is looking forward to retiring. Although, I am confident Nelson and Wyatt could operate the store without any supervision now."

"I agree," Celestia said as Landry nuzzled her head and pressed fervent kisses on her crown. "Orion plans on bringing his wife to England to visit next year. I cannot wait to meet her. She's part Mahican. Who knows, maybe he will decide to stay too. If not, I hope we can visit him in Vermont one day."

"I would like that," Landry said as a raven swooped down to land near the pond. After cocking its head and inspecting the area, it toddled forth and enjoyed a drink of the cool water. "I have always wanted to visit the United States. I admire the ingenuity and independence of her people. They remind me of a certain bluestocking."

Twisting to look up at him, Celestia bent her mouth into a loving smile. "You see me as something much more brilliant and courageous than I am, dear husband."

"Never," he countered. "You are a wonder, and I shall love you until the day I leave this world."

Turning in his embrace, Celestia kissed his square chin, then his firm mouth. "I shall love you until time ceases and beyond."

Want a FREE first in series Starter Library

from Collette?

Go to: signup.collettecameron.com/TheRegencyRoseGift

to get a five FREE book bundle.

EARL OF RENSHAW
For the Love of an Earl, Book Four

From *USA Today* bestselling author Collette Cameron comes a tantalizing tale of lies, scandal, and unexpected love with her latest Wicked Earls Club installment. A brooding earl and a desperate lady embark on a chaotic, humorous, romantic journey in this historical romance gem.

The dratted bounder mistook her for a runaway servant...
~Enemies to Lovers
~Class Difference
~Forced Proximity
~Rescued Heroine
~Fake Engagement
~Opposites Attract

~**Redeemed Rogue**
~**Cinderellaesque**
~**Second Chance**

When honor and destiny collide, scandal is never far behind…

Grace Dooley didn't mean to cause a scandal. She only wanted to escape her employer's son and his unwanted advances. Running into a terrible storm—ill and feverish, no less—would've never been part of her plan. Neither would getting caught hiding in a proper lord's coach. Blurting out that he was her betrothed? Also not on the agenda. But, oh, she did it. *All* of it…

Sanford Brockman, Earl of Renshaw, had avoided rumors and dishonor his entire life. Until a wretched (but undeniably pretty) woman made a public spectacle of him. But even though he *refuses* to go along with her ridiculous ruse, he can't abandon her—especially after she faints in his arms. All he can do now is help her recover—and hope his reputation can withstand the storm...

It's not long before Sanford learns there's more to Grace than meets the eye, and Grace discovers a charming soft side beneath Sanford's brooding exterior. But is mutual respect and attraction enough to put these polar opposites on the road to happily ever after? Or will society rip them apart forever?

USA Today Bestselling author COLLETTE CAMERON® is renowned for her Scottish and Regency historical romance novels featuring daring rogues, scoundrels, and the strong heroines who capture their hearts. Her stories are filled with inspiration and humor, making them the perfect escape for fans of Sweet-to-Spicy Timeless Romances®. Living in Oregon, Collette is a confessed Cadbury chocoholic and dreams of spending part of her time in Scotland. From the rugged highlands to the refined drawing rooms of Regency England, Collette's stories transport you to another time and place, where love and adventure are just a page away.

Thank you for reading EARL OF KEYWORTH.

Landry is my third wicked earl for the *Wicked Earls' Club* and *For the Love of an Earl Series*. My first two wicked earls were EARL OF WAINTHORPE and EARL OF SCARBOROUGH. Those wicked earls are also connected to my SEDUCTIVE SCOUNDRELS SERIES.

If you've read the other books in the SEDUCTIVE SCOUNDRELS SERIES, you've seen Landry mentioned a few times. A bit of a nonconformist, I wanted him to have a heroine that was a little outside the typical wife for a peer. In a period when women were greatly restricted, she made the most of her situation. I admire Celestia for her intrepidness.

Read the other *For the Love of an Earl* books:

EARL OF WAINTHORPE

EARL OF SCARBOROUGH

EARL OF RENSHAW

To make sure you do not miss any of my books, subscribe to *The Regency Rose*, my newsletter (Get a free book too!). I also have a fabulous VIP Reader

Group on Facebook. If you are a fan of my books and historical romance, I'd love to have you join me. You'll also be the first to see new covers, read exclusive excerpts, be the first to know about contests and giveaways, help me pick titles and name characters, and much, much more!

Please consider telling other readers why you enjoyed this book by reviewing it. I also truly adore hearing from my readers. You can contact me on my website and while you are there, explore my author world. If you enjoyed reading Landry and Celestia's story, be sure to check out the other books in my SEDUCTIVE SCOUNDRELS SERIES.

Hugs,

Collette